Bitter anger that Madeline should have her at such a disadvantage made Carol's voice harsh. "Researching people's my job."

"Well, it's mine too."

Carol thought, Did you dig up everything? That I fell in love with a woman, left my influential husband, abandoned my son? What a pretty story that would make for your bloody program. She said disdainfully, "unless you're intending to do an exposé of my life, you did it out of curiosity."

"You're angry with me?"

Carol said, her tone flat, "I'm furious."

Madeline leaned forward, put her hand on Carol's arm and said persuasively, "Carol, I'm not going to announce on air that you're living in a lesbian relationship."

"Thanks be for such mercies."

Madeline looked genuinely surprised at her bitter tone. "I thought we were friends . . ."

Are you doing this for sport? thought Carol. She drained her drink, stood up, put the glass down with a crack on the polished table. She felt like making threats, taking Madeline Shipley by the throat, breaking something.

Instead, she walked calmly out of the room, closing the door firmly behind her.

DEATH
DOWN UNDER

CLAIRE McNAB

DEATH
DOWN UNDER

CLAIRE McNAB

The Naiad Press, Inc.
1990

Printed in the United States of America
First Edition

Edited by Katherine V. Forrest
Cover design by Pat Tong and Bonnie Liss
    (Phoenix Graphics)
Typeset by Sandi Stancil

Library of Congress Cataloging-in-Publication Data

McNab, Claire.
    Death down under: a Detective Inspector Carol Ashton
mystery/by Claire McNab.
    I. Title.
PS3563.C3877D4   1989   813'.54   88-29120
ISBN 0-941483-39-8 (pbk.)

For Jo

About the Author

Claire McNab lives with her life partner and a menagerie of two German shepherds and two tortoise-shell cats in the beautiful northern beaches area of Sydney, Australia. She is the author of *Lessons in Murder* and *Fatal Reunion,* both featuring Detective Inspector Carol Ashton.

Acknowledgement

Katherine V. Forrest's editorial contribution to *Death Down Under* has been — to use a cliche she would never allow — simply the best!

Chapter 1

Detective Inspector Carol Ashton and Detective Sergeant Mark Bourke stood inside the fluttering blue and white plastic tape that marked the boundaries of the immediate scene of the crime. Ignoring the subdued bustle around them, they looked down at the body laid out so precisely at their feet.

"Poor kid," said Bourke. His pleasant face was professionally blank, but his voice betrayed his feelings.

He glanced at Carol. "It's the same one, Carol. We've got to get this guy."

"Guy? That makes him sound like one of the boys."

Her tone was mild, but he looked at her sharply. She was staring at the young woman lying in the muddy factory yard as though intent on imprinting the image into her mind. The hood over the victim's head, the naked body, the hands carefully arranged across her chest in a travesty of religious piety, the legs extended, placed together, the big toes neatly linked with a loop of orange cord to stop the feet from falling apart. Clothes had been folded in a tidy pile beside her left knee.

Bourke cleared his throat. "Same as the other three," he said, breaking the taut silence between them.

"No chance of a copycat?"

"It's him. As usual we haven't released all the details. No copycat murderer is going to get it exactly right."

Carol looked directly at him. She was his mentor, his friend, but her green eyes were as impersonal as glass. "You're not doing enough, Mark. He's still loose."

"Inspector?" The young uniformed officer was respectful. "The media . . . will you speak to them?"

Carol dismissed his diffident request with a nod, her eyes still on Bourke. "This *guy*," she said bitingly, "can't be allowed to do this again. Okay?"

Sybil Quade was curled up in a redwood patio chair catching the last warmth of the day's spring sunshine with a purring Jeffrey for company. She frowned over an untidy page of scrawled writing, red pen poised for corrections, yawning as she tried to concentrate on an interminable sentence whose recurring feature was an irritating use of "and then . . ." It was much more tempting to let her gaze shift to the soothing expanse of Middle Harbour lying in green-blue stillness far below the deck.

Rising at four that morning to be on the film set at five had made the day stretch to fatiguing length, and her efforts to supervise the education of two young students, who were much more eager to be out in front of the cameras than cramped around a table in a small motor caravan, had been even more tiring today than usual. She wondered wryly if the education authorities had any idea of the irrelevance of their detailed regulations for teaching in such situations. In essence she felt herself a glorified babysitter rather than a tutor, her duties being to provide a convincing picture of continuing education despite the demands of filming, while keeping her two young charges conveniently corralled so that they could be instantly located for wardrobe, make-up, or script rehearsal.

She looked up, smiling, as a small flock of rainbow lorikeets, intent on animated gossip, arrived with a flurry in the gumtree branches arching over the deck. She had often wondered why the strident colors of each bird — feathers of green, orange, yellow, blue and violet and a beak of bright red — did not create the expected clash, but complemented each other in delightful harmony. The only discordant note was struck by the rainbow lorikeet voice, which each bird employed in a stream of raucous comment.

The lorikeets attacked the insignificant pale pink

stamens that sprouted from the gumnuts, stuffing their beaks and talking at the same time. They were not tidy eaters, and Sybil protested as she was showered with a dusting of pink pieces. This galvanized Jeffrey into hunting mode. He gazed fixedly at the jewelled birds above him, his jaw working with a yah yah yah of anticipation.

Sybil admonished him, scooped him up under one arm and took both his reluctant self and her marking inside. As the sun rapidly faded, so did the spring warmth. She put her forehead against the huge plate glass window and took a last look at the harbor. Sometimes she missed her own house, situated so the ocean could be seen in its relentless attack upon the land, but today she welcomed the still water's tranquility because it matched her growing contentment.

It was now a year since she had rented out her house and moved in here with Carol. It had been a time of irrevocable changes both in her outward and her inner life. In many ways she could hardly recognize the person she had been two years ago — a woman cocooned by the structures and certainties of her society, where the pressures of conformity always made it more comfortable to follow unthinkingly than to question.

Now she found herself questioning everything, and not always finding a direction, let alone an answer. Even so, she was pushing against her own boundaries, growing in confidence and audacity, relishing the freedom she had never before realized she lacked.

Jeffrey stretched and yawned, triggering the same response in Sybil. She turned on the television to

4

catch the news, leaving it murmuring in the background as she concentrated on writing a helpful, rather than caustic, comment at the end of an untidy page.

She looked up at the clear tones of Carol's unmistakable voice, using the remote control to turn up the volume. Sybil had seen her interviewed many times, but the fascination never faded. She smiled at the face on the screen, admiring Carol's sleek blonde hair and marked bone structure. Her smile faded as she listened to Carol answering the questions fired at her at an impromptu media conference outside the rusty metal gates of a seedy factory. Yes, the body was that of a young woman . . . Her name couldn't be released until she was formally identified, but the family had been contacted . . . Yes, there were certain similarities with other cases involving the murder of other women . . . It was too early to say if she was the victim of a serial killer . . .

A male television reporter was scathingly persistent. Wasn't it true that the police had no leads, but four bodies? Why wouldn't she admit it was the Orange Strangler again? Why weren't the police using the latest scientific advances to track down this monster? How many young women had to be slaughtered before something positive was done?

Carol listened patiently, eyes intent upon her questioner, ignoring the microphones thrust in her face by the urgent enthusiasm of other media representatives. When his questions trailed off, she answered with calm courtesy, pointing out that it seemed likely that victims were chosen by the murderer at random, thus making it extremely difficult to predict where the person might strike next. "We are making an appeal to the general public," she said, "to contact the police with any information that might have any bearing at all on this series of murders. We will be setting up a special line to handle these calls, but in the meantime, please ring your local police station."

The reporter was still belligerent. "What about genetic fingerprinting, Inspector Ashton? Doesn't the Police Department want to use these advanced techniques, or do they cost too much? Is that it?"

Carol's response was in her usual reasonable tone. "The New South Wales police force has access to the latest scientific developments in forensic science, particularly in the field you mention, DNA profiling. In a case like this, however, because the murderer could be anyone in the general population, the application of these new techniques is limited."

Carol's face disappeared, to be replaced by a long shot of weeping parents being ushered into a car. Sybil grimaced at the pitiless invasion of private grief, switching channels to catch Carol on another newscast.

This time Carol was pictured with Mark Bourke inside the half-open rusty gate in the factory fence. "Detective Inspector Carol Ashton," said the voice-over portentously, "abruptly taken off the politically sensitive Moreno case to stalk the Orange Strangler. Is this, as some are saying, a panic move on the part of the Commissioner of Police? An open admission that the forces of law and order are no closer to catching this killer than they were when he struck a year ago?"

There followed a montage of images of the first three victims with the announcer describing with

6

emphatic outrage the rising tide of fear that, he assured viewers, "gripped the city!"

Sybil punched the off button as a plump male psychologist began to explain in self-important tones how the hatred of women could fester until it burst into stylized violence.

Carol shut the door of her office with unusual vehemence, cutting off the irritation of ringing telephones and her colleagues' banter. She was quite aware that the smothering tiredness she felt was not caused by fatigue alone, but by the effort to suppress an incandescent anger. The persistent reporter's words came back to her: *How many young women have to be slaughtered* . . . Why was so much violence directed at women by males who beat, raped, and even killed as though it was their right to do so?

She rubbed her forehead, looked at her watch and, with a sigh of resignation, dialed a number. "Sybil? It's me. Darling, I'm sorry, but I'm going to be late again. Don't wait up, okay?" She smiled at the affectionate protest at the other end. "Well, it's partly your fault for romping off to your film set at such ridiculous times. I'll get home as soon as I can. Yes, all right, I promise to wake you if I'm not too late."

Carol replaced the receiver and sat gazing with unfocused eyes at the black opal ring on her left hand. She wanted to get up, walk out and go home to Sybil. To slam shut her mind, turn off her imagination, ignore the world of lust and violence she was supposed to deal with impartially every day.

What could shock her now? In her career she had seen the worst that one human being could do to another — so what was one more senseless addition to the hundred or so murders committed in New South Wales every year? Apart from gang warfare, the small number of murderous citizens of the Premier State were generally inclined to exterminate their nearest and dearest. Not perfect strangers. Not young women who had done them no harm.

Over the last few months Carol had been fully occupied with the shotgun murder of a colleague, Inspector Morena. His death had been the impetus for a series of allegations about police corruption and drug ring payoffs, so Carol, because she enjoyed a consistently favorable reception from the media, had been brought in to handle the investigation.

Her acerbic comment to the Commissioner that it almost seemed as if the investigation was to be eclipsed by public relations and that what the press and television portrayed was of more value than the facts themselves, had brought a quick response: "Carol, they trust you out there. They know you won't be party to a cover-up. You're straight. You tell it like it is."

She had smiled wryly at his comments. His use of the word "straight" had been as unintentionally ironic as his conviction that she wouldn't agree to a cover-up. Hadn't she done everything she could to keep her relationship with Sybil separate and secret — to use, if necessary, lies and evasions to hide the truth?

In her professional life she was accustomed to the glare of publicity. Critical though she was of the media, sometimes she would admit to herself that she could, on occasion, enjoy the limelight and gain satisfaction from her performance in a difficult interview. The public relations associated with the investigation into Inspector Morena's death had been an unwelcome challenge, but one she had found unexpectedly exhilarating.

Now the Morena case was being wound up. The Commissioner had been relieved at Carol's findings: the murder was quite unconnected with drug dealings, and the result of a psychotic minor crook's major grudge against his arrest and conviction some years before.

"Brief Bradley so he can tidy up the loose ends," he had said two days ago, "because I want you directly involved in the serial strangler case. We've been upping the reward and getting nowhere, Carol. Solving this sort of crime relies a lot on luck, I know, but we're copping a lot of flack from the public. You can have anything you want, within reason. But I want action, fast."

The first victim of the man the press had now cheerfully dubbed "The Orange Strangler" had been Maria Kelly. She had died almost a year ago, near Christmas when Carol had been on vacation.

The circumstances of this first murder had been unusual enough to generate publicity for a few days, but it took the second death six months later in May to really catch the media's attention. Sally-Jean Cross was one of their own, an investigative journalist who specialized in what might charitably be called "the human interest behind the headline," although her activities had more pungently been described by a media critic as "ruthless exploitation of the tragic victims of disaster and violence."

9

The irony of Sally-Jean becoming a headline herself was not lost upon her colleagues, and in-depth profiles of her career — and sensational suggestions that perhaps a story she had covered in the past had led to her gruesome end — ran side-by-side with the details of her already well-publicized relationship with a wealthy media baron, Wilbur Shearing.

At the time of Sally-Jean's death she had just been discarded by him for someone younger and more photogenic. Skating as close to the stringent defamation laws as possible, those news services not in his media stable slyly commented on the timing of her demise, which had conveniently occurred just one week before she was to appear on a popular television talk program to discuss her private life and experiences.

The police having made no apparent progress on these first two murders, the publicity eventually died down, flaring up again three months later with victim three, Narelle Dent.

And last night, less than two months later, the fourth murder, identical in every respect.

She picked up the handset decisively. "Mark, I'm on my way to your office. I want to go through everything you've got, from the basics right through to where you are right now."

Chapter 2

Mark Bourke looked weary. His colleagues often joked about his almost obsessive personal neatness, which was reflected in the tidiness of his office, but tonight he was sprawled in his chair with his shirtsleeves rolled up and his tie loosened. Even his short, smooth brown hair was ruffled.

Carol was suddenly struck by the power in his forearms. Physical force was not something she usually associated with Bourke. They had worked together on many cases and she had come to take for granted his unobtrusive efficiency, but now she looked speculatively at his blunt-featured, pleasant face, aware that she knew little of his private life. She remembered some casual reference to a personal tragedy that had occurred several years before she had first worked with him — the loss of his wife and child in a boating accident. He had never mentioned it to her.

It's absurd, she thought, to choose this moment to worry about Mark's personal life. Even so, she felt a moment's guilt. He had been a supportive friend to her in the past . . . what had she given in return?

"Okay," she said briskly, "what've you got?"

Mark Bourke's voice was flat and tired, his usual humorous tone absent. "The cord around the neck, it's always the same stuff. Bright orange six millimeter eight-strand plaited nylon."

Carol fingered the sample he handed her. "Unusual in any way?"

"Nope. And easy to obtain from a range of outlets, so there's not much hope of tracing anything there. The knot's a bit more interesting. Same one each time and neatly tied. It's a type of modified clove hitch called, rather appropriately, a constrictor knot."

"Is it used in any particular trade or activity?"

"Not really. Could be someone who's interested in boating, sailing, that sort of thing." He tried to smile to loosen her tight face. "Boy Scouts like to tie knots. Perhaps we're chasing a maddened scoutmaster."

Carol's detached expression didn't change. She said, "Why use this particular knot?"

"Well, it's called a constrictor knot because it gets tighter and tighter as load is applied to the ends, and remains just as tight when the pressure is removed. It isn't, however, ideal for strangling, since it needs a couple of loops around the neck and the ends have to pass underneath to complete the knot. As far as we can work it out, he half-throttles the woman with a single loop, and when she's unconscious he takes his time to tie a neat final constrictor knot to finish the job."

Her mouth tightened, but her voice held only a note of interested inquiry. "Are they drugged in any way?"

"No drugs. The second one, Sally-Jean Cross, had traces of alcohol in her blood, as did Narelle Dent, but in each case it wasn't much. They certainly weren't drunk. Don't know about the one last night, but the first victim, Maria Kelly, was cold hard sober, so there's no reason she'd obligingly stand still while he tied an elaborate knot around her throat. Anyway, the post mortems suggest our theory of pre-strangling is probably right."

Her tone was caustic. "Pre-strangling, Mark? Sounds like an exciting little foreplay before murder."

"Carol, this one's really got to you. I don't know why —"

"Go on with the m.o."

Bourke made a face. "He's a tidy bastard. As you saw today, he arranges the bodies to a pattern and every time it's the same. Each victim's been found lying on her back in a parody of the laying out of the dead with her arms bent and crossed over her chest, her legs straight with the feet together. Of course, our boy adds his own little touches — the head's covered by a hood, in each case a cheap cotton pillowslip, and he ties the thumbs together to prevent

13

the crossed-over arms separating. Does the same with the big toes to keep the feet together. Makes for a neat corpse."

"What sort of knots for the hands and feet?"

"Same orange cord and nothing fancy as far as the knot's concerned. Just an ordinary reef knot with the ends tucked under."

"The pillowcase?"

"Absolutely nothing to trace. Each one's new, made of white cotton and mass-produced."

Carol moved her shoulders impatiently, her skin whispering against the blue silk of her blouse. "Then what have you got?"

"Not much. No similars in other states. No reliable eye-witness accounts."

"Any likelys?"

"No. We've run through all the known sex offenders in each state — also international — with no result. The only one with a modus operandi anything like this is safely locked up in South Australia, and even he wasn't as kinky as this guy."

Her sharp tone mirrored her brittle anger. "So you're telling me you've got four bodies and no suspects. Is that right?"

He turned his palms to her, his face creased with the frustration she realized he would usually hide. "Carol, you know how hard these are. Sure, we've had the usual confessions from the loonies, the telephone calls from people who just know their next door neighbor's a mass murderer, the revenge calls — and everything's been checked out. We've had a couple of leads that looked promising at the time — identikit faces went to the media for a possible suspect seen near where Sally-Jean Cross was dumped

14

and again for Narelle Dent, but not only was there no similarity between the two illustrations, we eventually traced both of them and there was no way either was involved."

Regretting her anger, she said in a more moderate tone, "Sally-Jean Cross was heavily involved with Wilbur Shearing. Did he check out okay?"

"How could you doubt it, Carol?" he said sourly. "When Wilbur Shearing the Second says he's clean, all his newspapers and television stations agree with him."

"Is he?"

Bourke turned down the corners of his mouth. "Looks like it, more's the pity. Surrounded himself with a battalion of legal eagles the moment Sally-Jean's identity was out, but I imagine that'd be normal practice for someone like him if there was trouble in the offing."

"Alibi?"

"Of course. We investigated him pretty thoroughly, but unfortunately he came up clean. Even so, I've got Ferguson checking his movements last night. After his ex-girlfriend's death we gently suggested he might like to volunteer a blood sample for DNA profiling, but he told us to go jump and we had no other evidence to force the issue. Couldn't even find out his blood group as he's not the sort to be a blood donor and he doesn't appear to have ever had surgery where blood typing was done."

Carol flipped over the pages of the report on Sally-Jean's death. "What've you got to tie Shearing to the scene if you do persuade him to give a tissue sample?"

Bourke leaned back in his chair, hands behind his

15

head, and stared morosely at the ceiling. "We can't tie him to Sally-Jean direct. There were some clothing fibers on her hands and she probably ripped his shirt, but anyone would have got rid of incriminating clothing straight away. The best we could hope for is to match him up with the skin under the fingernails of the first woman, Maria Kelly. She apparently reached back as she was being strangled and scratched her attacker pretty badly, so we know he's type O Positive blood."

"How about semen?"

"None. There's no rape — in fact no sexual assault of any kind."

"The third victim, Narelle Dent — anything there?"

Bourke sat up straight, saying matter-of-factly, "He was improving in efficiency with her. Not a thing except for fragments of orange nylon where she tried to loosen the cord. Other than that she didn't seem to put up much of a fight at all."

Carol had a sudden vivid picture of a length of orange cord abruptly looping over her head, biting into her throat, cutting off her air and her life. How many women would have the presence of mind to go for the attacker, not the rope that was throttling them?

She said, "When do we get the info on this last one?"

Bourke shrugged. "I've pulled every string I can. They say they'll do their best."

"Not good enough," said Carol, picking up his phone. "I want a full report first thing tomorrow morning, and I don't care how many people have to stay up all night to do it."

* * * * *

Driving home through the late night loneliness
was always disorienting to Carol. The city streets,
swarming with life during the hours of light, seemed
to become at night the territory of the feral and the
dispossessed. Huge metal vehicles crawled along, water
gushing and motorized brooms sweeping the grime
and rubbish of the day away, the clank of machinery
and the voices of their operators loud in the echoing
silence.

The Harbour Bridge still hummed with life and
light and she often wondered why all these people
were out so late and to what destinations they so
single-mindedly drove.

After she left the main arteries the volume of
traffic dropped dramatically, but at this time of night
the few vehicles were driven faster and with more
determination.

She entered into an inadvertent contest with a
BMW on the double bends of Spit Road, and,
suddenly fired with competitiveness, she raced him
down the long hill, across Spit Bridge spanning the
metallic moonlit water and up the steep pull on the
other side.

She grinned and waved an acknowledging hand as
she slowed to turn off to the left and he roared
victoriously ahead. She whipped along the quiet
streets, alert for suicidal cats or possums, and finally
turned into her street-level double carport.

A gibbous moon swam in a dark sky, creating a
black and silver world of alien shadows and
unfamiliar surfaces. Sinker, tail up, met her as she
walked down the path to the house; he was closely

17

followed by Sybil's chubby Jeffrey. Sinker had not been a gracious cat when Jeffrey had moved in a year ago, but his feline surliness had been somewhat tempered by time, and he now regarded the ginger interloper with an air of superior indifference.

"I know Sybil fed you hours ago," said Carol as the two cats ambitiously portrayed joint starvation. "So don't waste your time with me." She knew, as did they, that she would give them late supper, but she always put up a token show of resistance.

Sybil had left the light on in the living room. Its blond furniture, bright rugs and pale cedar walls were familiar and comforting. Carol put her briefcase by the bench separating the room from the spacious kitchen, told the cats to be patient, and went into the bedroom. Sybil was asleep. Carol leaned over her. "I'm home, darling," she said, and watched her stir and murmur indistinctly. Carol was stabbed with a sudden fear for Sybil's vulnerability. A woman, alone, sleeping. What could protect her from attack? Statistics? Luck?

Carol moved her tight shoulders. Most people thought it would never happen to them, and it generally didn't — but she saw the victims, the unlucky ones, whose lives had been destroyed because of the fatal conjunction of time, place and intent, that bizarre linking of predator and victim.

She touched Sybil's cheek, then went back to the kitchen and the briefcase holding the stark details of the lives and deaths of three young women and the preliminary details on Alissa Harvey, who had been positively identified by her distraught parents late that afternoon.

Sinker and Jeffrey greeted their light fish supper

18

with the usual expressions of hauteur at both the content and the size of the portions. She smiled at their ritual disdain, poured herself a whiskey and water, and placed the folders in a neat row along the bench.

Lives reduced to a file with a printed designation in the right-hand corner: MARIA KELLY; SALLY-JEAN CROSS; NARELLE DENT. Alissa Harvey's existence had not yet shrunk to a name on a folder, but Mark Bourke would print one for her tomorrow.

She took a deep breath as she opened Maria Kelly's file. The young woman stared up at her with the smiling confidence of one believing time was on her side. It was a publicity still — she had had a few small parts in advertisements and a couple of walk-on roles in television soap operas. Perhaps coincidentally, the last program she had appeared in was telecast by Wilbur Shearing's Sydney channel.

Carol stared at the open face soberly. Maria Kelly: twenty-three, aspiring actor, healthy, probably happy, and now dead because she was selected to be the first victim of a serial killer.

But how was she chosen? Why? Was there a pattern? Somewhere in the mystery of her personality, in her activities, her friends, even her looks? Was it as simple as the fact that he hated women, and she was available to kill? But if so, what triggered the murder? A sexual advance from the victim that so revolted him he had to snuff out the person who made it? Or was it some perverted religious fervor that had been translated into a series of sacrifices to a god who demanded blood?

Maria Kelly had died a year ago, in December,

19

with Christmas decorations in the shops and the warmth of summer bursting into each day. Long experience had made Carol accustomed to the photographs of violent crime, but even she winced at the contrast between the pretty smiling face and the contorted features revealed when the pillowslip had been removed. Her body had been found at Audley Weir in the Royal National Park to the south of Sydney, a huge area of natural bushland, perfect for a hasty grave. But no attempt had been made to conceal the naked corpse, which had been neatly arranged in a parody of respect for death in picnic grounds beside the Port Hacking River.

She skim-read the details: death from asphyxiation ten to twelve hours before the discovery of the body; lividity indicated that the body had been left lying on its side for some time before being arranged on its back; a meal of Chinese food had been eaten about an hour before death; blood samples showed no trace of alcohol.

Carol grimaced. Going clear-headed to one's end: was it better to know what was happening — to keenly feel those last moments of life — or was it better to be lost in an alcoholic haze so that all the edges of terror were blunted?

Maria Kelly's clothes had been carefully folded and placed close to the bare feet of her body, together with her leather handbag with papers and money intact. Mark Bourke had written in pencil in the margin of the report, *Knows how to fold things so they won't crush — neat at packing. Sells clothes? Travels a lot?*

The next pages gave a minute breakdown of all the personal details of Maria Kelly's life. Death had removed both her life and her right to privacy. Information about the web of connections in which everyone moves: family, friends, acquaintances, workmates — the people who may like, love, hate or be indifferent to you. And, of course, details of Maria Kelly's sexual experience. Would she have blushed to read the cold analysis of her private world? She had been moderately active, apparently emotionally uninvolved. No conveniently jealous boyfriend was available as a suspect, no unusual secret activity provided a motive. She was an ordinary, attractive, unremarkable girl who had dreamed of fame as an actor and had achieved the glare of publicity, not by her talents, but by the manner of her murder.

Carol swallowed the last of her whiskey in one gulp, set the glass down deliberately, turned out the light and walked out onto the moonlit deck. Silvered gumtrees sighed in a gentle wind, the maddening *koo-well* call of the elusive bird, a koel, repeated over and over. He was establishing his territory, using the cooler night air to carry his message to any would-be rivals. Birds, animals — they didn't rape and kill. They didn't indulge in rituals with purpose only to satisfy a hidden sickness.

"You bastard," she said to the night. "Are you sleeping soundly now? I'm going to find you, wherever you are."

Chapter 3

Sybil had given a cursory glance to the morning paper with its screaming headlines about the latest victim of the Orange Strangler, and she was now squinting over the rim of a strong cup of coffee at the yellow call sheet for Day Ten of *Death Down Under*. It listed the scenes to be shot that day, giving exhaustive details of crew requirements, locations, parking, catering, and when and where each actor was required to appear. The movie was set in the fifties, so street scenes had to avoid the burgeoning development of modern Sydney. Today the location shots were in the old suburb of Glebe, and Sybil's two young charges were required for early scenes from 7:30 a.m. onwards. Although she wasn't responsible for their arrival on the set, she was expected to be available to keep each of them under benign surveillance and to cajole them, when they were free from shooting, into some attempt at learning to make up for the schoolwork they were missing.

Sybil found the youngest, an Aboriginal girl, Kirra Goolamurra, delightfully effervescent and eager. Malcolm Murtry, her white co-star, presented more of a challenge. His attitude was one of self-important surliness, partly because he apparently perceived himself as a nascent sex symbol of the intense variety and partly because he clearly resented that a rising star of his caliber should have to waste time on schoolwork.

Apart from the difficulties of imparting any meaningful education on a film set, Sybil was enjoying herself enormously. For one thing she had been fascinated to meet Ripley Patterson in the flesh, the imported American movie star whose almost indecently handsome face was as familiar as a next door neighbor's. His presence was a guarantee of movie distribution rights in the States.

In addition to such brushes with fame, Sybil also found it exhilarating to be part of a cooperative effort involving so many people expert in so many different fields, working seamlessly together with one aim: to create a movie. She had already developed an easy relationship with sound and lighting, shared jokes with catering, and listened, fascinated, to show business gossip in wardrobe and make-up. She was intrigued by the god-like status of the director, Vic Carbond, whose two assistant directors passed on his messages as if delivered from on high — instructions, commands and comments that were faithfully relayed to the team of people swarming around each scene.

When the company was not in the studio, but shooting on location, all equipment, including a generator, had to be brought to the site, and departments such as wardrobe and make-up had to organize separate trailers. Sybil particularly admired the achievements of Charlie Date, who, as principal unit manager, was responsible for organizing all movements of the entire crew from place to place during shooting as well as controlling traffic, providing parking and making sure that that most vital of departments, catering, was available on schedule.

She glanced at her watch. Traffic at 6:30 a.m. was generally light, but she had to be sure to be at the Glebe location well on time. She went quietly into the bedroom. Carol lay on her back, one slim tanned arm flung up above her head, blonde hair across the dark blue pillow, her sculptured face unguarded. The firm lines of her mouth relaxed, she looked younger, softer. Sybil reflected that they were always leaving each other asleep. Carol was working ridiculously long hours, while she herself had taken time off full-time teaching for this eight week contract with Mayberry Movies, an offshoot of Wilbur Shearing's media empire.

She wanted to slide back into bed with Carol, but instead she touched the pale hair with one finger and bent to kiss her goodbye. Carol stirred, opened her green eyes, smiled. Her voice was husky with sleep.

24

"Do you have to go so early? Stay with me a bit longer."

"Can't. *Death Down Under* calls. But don't forget you promised you'd be home at a reasonable hour tonight. I'll see you then."

Carol reached up, put her arms around Sybil's neck and pulled her down into an embrace. Her mouth was warm, her tongue insistent. She slid her hands under Sybil's top, her fingernails gently grazing the skin of her back.

Sybil broke away laughing. "Oh no you don't! You can't seduce me that easily. But don't be discouraged. You will try again tonight?"

"If you're very lucky — maybe."

She was reluctant to leave. She had begun to miss their usual routine where they shared the day's experiences, often with warmth and laughter but sometimes with darker emotions. Suddenly serious, she said, "Carol, is everything all right?"

Carol smothered a yawn. "Sure. See you tonight."

As Sybil joined the early morning traffic, she was frowning. She was used to Carol's withdrawal when she was on a challenging case — yet there was a sense of brittleness about her reserve this time. If there was only time to talk . . . But being together was a luxury at the moment.

Since the terms of Sybil's contract required her presence when her students were in attendance, this meant she worked to an irregular pattern that varied from day to day, and often changed during the course of shooting, especially when weather altered plans for scenes on location outside the studio. At the end of the next week the entire unit, including her and her two students, would leave Sydney, traveling to Ayers

25

Rock and the surrounding red desert areas. As she had said mockingly to Carol, "As far as I can see, the plot of *Death Down Under* isn't really riveting, the acting's not that crash hot — but the scenery, Carol! Now *that's* going to be great!"

The suburb of Glebe was situated near the august presence of Sydney University, and students searching for shared accommodations close to lectures had invaded Glebe's compact houses and rows of terraces. Formerly a dormitory suburb supplying labor for commerce and industry, it was now home to a wide social range — students, executives, intellectuals, a core of working class salts-of-the-earth and — as in all cities — the dispossessed, for whom life was a cycle of poverty and disappointment.

When Sybil arrived at the junction of Bredon Street and Glebe Point Road most of the unit's vehicles were parked and the traffic barriers were up. Attentive bystanders loitered, alert for something to happen. Sybil felt like telling them not to bother. One thing she had discovered about movie-making was the interminable waiting between those short bursts of activity when part of the script was actually committed to film.

She parked a block away and walked up to the clump of trailers and trucks. Filming in Sydney streets demanded a combination of barefaced effrontery and a reliance on the curiosity of the general public. Permissions from the traffic authorities and local councils rarely covered the full range of activities of a film crew, and Sybil was constantly amazed at how far the good will of individuals could be stretched. Technicians tramped on gardens, parked across driveways, disrupted traffic, begged the use of toilet facilities and generally made themselves at home.

Her own small motor caravan, nicknamed the Education Express by the crew, had been parked under the drooping branches of a dispirited tree. Charlie Date, the unit manager, nodded to her and smiled a greeting as she opened the door. When they had first been introduced he hadn't wasted much time in pleasantries, but in the last few days he had, for him, been positively effusive.

She clambered into the restricted space of the caravan to put out the materials for the first session with her students, looking up as Charlie stuck his head through the door. He said, "I've put catering half way down Bredon Street. Your kids will be dropped there for breakfast. Better join them, eh?" His tone was pleasant, but had an accusatory effect, as though he were hinting she was being rather slack in her duties.

Looking at Charlie's opaque pale blue eyes, drooping brown mustache and neat dimpled chin, Sybil felt an unreasonable irritation. Although he was obviously warming to her, he still regarded her as an outsider, a stranger amid the team of people whose skills meshed together to produce a movie. They all talked to each other with an easy camaraderie born of many similar situations, a huge and shifting family whose members had one thing in common: the production of images on a screen.

Charlie waited while she shut the caravan door. "I'll walk down with you," he said.

He was large but not muscular, his voice just a little too high and a little too mild to match his bulk. She tried to think of a word to describe his physique

— not soft, not fat, but sleek, too well-covered, cushiony, with no hardness underneath.

To fill what she found to be an uncomfortable silence, she made a few light remarks as they walked along. Charlie obviously didn't believe in inconsequential chatter, as he merely nodded at appropriate intervals. His eyes, however, hardly left her face.

Alice Fleming, the wardrobe mistress, had already taken it upon herself to caution Sybil about Charlie Date. "Good man," she had said, "heart of gold, dear, but just recovering from a devastating divorce. Believe his wife left him for another woman, would you believe! *And* took the kids. He sees them of course — he's a good father. Takes them out on his boat every chance he gets. But I don't think he's ready for another relationship yet. I mean, his trust in women must have just been absolutely destroyed, mustn't it?"

Alice was an avid consumer of personal details which she collected with vacuum-cleaner efficiency. Her wide, thin-lipped mouth was never still — at one moment pursed with surprise, then agape in wonder at some hidden morsel she had uncovered. Her position as wardrobe mistress apparently provided her with unparalleled opportunities to gather such personal snippets and, thus armed, she presented herself as an authority on the varnished and unvarnished particulars of each person's life.

Sybil knew she was providing Alice with an unexpected challenge. Alice questioned, sometimes with sly indirection, sometimes with blunt directness, but, amused, Sybil parried each time. Unfazed, Alice would brush her brown crinkly hair back from her face and try again.

Charlie broke into Sybil's thoughts, saying abruptly, "Come out with me tonight? We're not shooting."

She hid her astonishment with a quick refusal. "I'm sorry Charlie, I'm tied up."

"Sybil's a woman of mystery," said another voice behind them.

Although Charlie frowned unwelcomingly, the intruder, Luke West, fell into step with them.

"You should know," he said cheerfully to Charlie, "that Syb sticks strictly to business. Even Alice Fleming's drawn a blank, and that would have to be a record!" He smiled at Sybil. "Come on," he said, "you can tell Charlie and me all about it. Just who is the man in your life?"

She wondered how they'd react to the truth. She'd told Carol that if anyone on the set asked her a direct question, she'd like to be able to answer it. She could still hear Carol's angry retort: "I don't want people discussing our personal life. It isn't anybody's business but ours."

She thought, If I'd been quite open in the beginning I wouldn't have this situation now.

"Honestly," she said, "my life's really quite boring. You wouldn't find it interesting at all."

Luke West smiled at her. Charlie Date didn't.

Carol tried to jog early every morning, but in the past few weeks pressure of work had meant she had not kept strictly to her routine. Collecting Olga, her neighbor's exuberant German shepherd, she pushed herself at a fast clip up the steeply inclined streets

29

around her house and through the neighboring bush reserve. It was later in the morning than she usually ran, and the sun had already developed a sting. Under the dappled shade of the gumtrees insects hummed in patterns of undulating sound, but the birds who called so ebulliently in the early morning were silent. Wattle bushes were bursting with their yellow balls and the tang of eucalyptus filled the warm air. Olga loped effortlessly beside her as she began to labor, but Carol refused to let herself slacken her pace. When she dropped Olga off and returned home breathless and aching with the effort, she felt renewed and strengthened because of the discipline she had imposed on herself.

The phone rang as she took off her running shoes. Mark Bourke's voice was buoyant. "Carol, you'll never guess, but Madeline Shipley claims she's had a phone call from someone who could be our man."

Carol sifted quickly through her memory. Madeline Shipley: one of the most successful of Australia's media personalities. *The Shipley Report* was strip-scheduled to run in the early evening, Monday to Friday. It enjoyed consistently high ratings and could best be described as soft current affairs. She didn't have to pursue her interviewees — they lined up to be on her show. "When?" said Carol.

"Last night, just after her program finished. It went to air live, as usual, and she says they often get a big telephone response to the show. Everyone watches it, so why not a serial killer? From what she says, I think there's a possibility it's genuine."

"One of us better see her."

"I'd love to subject myself to the Shipley charm,

but of course it's you she wants. She'll be available at ten this morning at the channel. Watch out she doesn't sign you to an exclusive deal. You know what she's like . . . . And Carol, one other thing — the program Sally-Jean was due to appear on before her untimely death just happened to be *The Shipley Report.* Interesting, eh?"

Carol was thoughtful as she replaced the receiver. Long experience with the media had accustomed her to the unspoken rules applying to the giving and receiving of favors. Cynically, she saw it as an elaborate game of mutual manipulation, with individuals in the media willing to be cooperative in return for special concessions regarding access and exclusivity.

Madeline Shipley, however, didn't play quite the same game. She stood above it, largely untouched by the wheeling and dealing. Married to an artist, she kept her own personal life totally private, but she gave of herself on the screen and her audience loved her for it. She was, of course, good-looking — television didn't reward females who failed the comeliness test — but there was more to her than physical beauty. Men and women alike were captivated by her charm, palpable as a warm and gentle breeze.

Carol had never appeared on this particular program, but, watching Madeline Shipley on the screen, she had often felt the pull of that formidable charm. Of course, Carol thought sardonically, that was exactly why she was so successful. With relaxed skill she would interview a pompous politician, a "personality," or some ordinary person enjoying fleeting fame until the next news story came along, and in each case with gentle, almost ruefully probing questions, Madeline Shipley focused on the personal. It was amazing how much she could encourage people to reveal about themselves, all apparently without resort to artifice or trickery.

But not me, thought Carol as she changed from her running clothes. You're never going to get to the core of me.

Madeline Shipley shook hands, briefly, firmly. "Detective Inspector Ashton. How good of you to make time to see me."

"My duty, surely, since you have, I presume, valuable information for us?"

Madeline Shipley grinned at the irony in her voice. "Don't be on your guard against me, Inspector . . . or may I call you Carol?"

Carol's tone was dry. "By all means. Am I then to call you Madeline?"

"Please."

Wary but amused, Carol took the seat offered to her. Madeline Shipley's office was large and sumptuous, as befitted a star of her magnitude, and it was almost certainly more luxurious than those of the television executives who employed her. The theme colors were beige and blue, and the hand of an interior decorator of style had ordered a blue plush carpet of deepest pile, set the expensive dark blue leather couches and chairs in a casually intimate circle, and hung a tasteful oil on the pale beige wallpaper. One wall was made of glass, looking out onto a courtyard filled with greenery and the liquid tracery of a small but forceful fountain.

As Madeline ordered coffee for them both, Carol attempted a dispassionate assessment. In the flesh Madeline was even more attractive than on the screen. She wore an understated but exquisitely cut pale gray suit and no jewelry. She was slightly built, coming barely to Carol's shoulder. Her long copper hair gleamed, her wide gray eyes, fringed with the requisite long dark lashes, were full of easy laughter, her mouth curved in a smile. Carol wanted to arm herself with dislike, but found it impossible.

It's her particular talent, thought Carol, vexed with herself. She wants to disarm me by making me feel that at this moment I'm the only important and fascinating person in her life.

She had wasted enough time on preliminaries. Carol asked, "When did you get this call and what makes you think it isn't just another crank?"

"Last night, after the show. And it didn't have the feel of the usual crank call. Believe me, I'd know."

Carol raised an eyebrow. "I imagine a lot of loonies try to get to you. Why are you answering your own calls?"

"I usually don't. You're right, of course, anyone in my business gets a few disturbed people pestering them from time to time. For that reason my assistant screens everyone who tries to get in touch with me.

Last night, just after we finished at seven-thirty, Helen took a call from a man. She thought I should speak to him, so I did."

"I'll need to speak to the assistant." If the call was genuine, she wanted as many impressions as possible about age, nationality and anything individualistic about his speaking voice. She said, "And what about the station's switchboard? I know they log calls. Is there any reason why an operator would remember this particular one?"

"I doubt it. We get a lot of public response after each show, especially if it's been controversial in some way. I'll get Helen to check who was on last night and see if we can get a copy of the logs. Then you can see Helen yourself."

Carol watched her pick up the receiver and give instructions. Was it really possible that she *was* as genuinely nice as she appeared? How much easier to be cynical and think her charm skin-deep. But she had an aura of sincerity that contradicted Carol's preferred assessment of a professionally pleasant but essentially superficial media personality.

She replaced the receiver, smiled at Carol. "You know, Carol, it's such a pleasure to meet you. I've admired your handling of my colleagues many times. Perhaps you should consider a career in television — there's certainly nothing you need to learn about dealing with the rigors of an interview."

"I adore flattery," said Carol, her derisive tone unmistakable.

Madeline was amused. "You think I'm trying to soften you up to get you on my show."

"Are you?"

"Not exactly. But if . . ."

"Right now I need to know everything about this call. Did you have any impression you'd heard his voice before?"

"It's hard to say. Not all voices are distinctive and anyway he was, I thought, putting on a broad Australian accent. I don't think he spoke that way normally."

"Are incoming calls ever taped?"

"Hardly, since it's not strictly legal. However I must admit in a few cases we have bent the rules and recorded individuals making specific threats. Most of the time if someone's abusive, or odd in some way, it's standard practice to try to get a name and address. Of course, people like that tend to want to be anonymous. A few times when we've had repeated threats the calls have been traced, but it's never been anything but some unhappy person with an imaginary ax to grind."

There was a sharp knock at the door. A young woman entered, power-dressed in a smart blue suit, an air of brisk promptitude about her.

"I'm Helen Tolsten, Madeline's personal assistant," she said before an introduction could be made. "Here's a copy of the telephone log from last night, as you requested, but I don't believe it'll be much help." As she handed the papers to Carol she added, "And I've included a transcript of the call I took as far as I can remember it."

While Carol was blinking at such efficiency, Helen said to Madeline, "You've an appointment at eleven.

35

I've prepared some background notes for you." She spoke with jerky rapidity, giving the impression she was anxious to finish as quickly as possible and hurry away.

"I would like to ask you a few questions," said Carol.

Madeline watched with a faint smile as Helen Tolsten sat down abruptly, concentrated her attention on Carol, and waited. Carol, a little amused, studied her for a moment. Slightly plump, impressively tailored, Helen gave an impression of controlled impatience. She had short brown hair in a no-nonsense style, dark direct eyes, a light dusting of make-up, no jewelry except a large-faced watch. She didn't fidget or move, yet looked as though she would leap from the chair with alacrity if given the chance.

Carol said, "I believe there are often a number of calls after a program and that you usually take them. Why did you pass this one on to Madeline?"

Helen didn't waste words. "Sounded genuine. Knew Madeline would want to deal with it herself."

"Can you give me an idea of his age and nationality?"

Helen didn't pause to consider. "Age? Bit hard to say. Not too old. Twenties, early thirties. And he was Australian. No doubt."

"Not putting on an Australian accent?"

"No."

Carol raised her eyebrows. "How can you be so positive? An actor could assume an accent."

Helen shrugged, obviously unwilling to waste her time arguing over a certainty.

Carol was finding her own voice slowing down in reaction to Helen's snapped syllables. She said, "Tell me about his voice. Was there anything different about it, either in tone or the way he used his words?"

"He was Australian," said Helen with emphasis, "but was exaggerating the accent. Made it broader than he'd usually speak. Can't think of anything else."

"Did you get an impression of his feelings? Was he nervous? Angry?"

Helen had obviously not expected this question; she paused before answering. "He was confident, sure of himself. One of the things that convinced me Madeline should speak to him."

Carol handed her back the transcript to read aloud. It was a short conversation and Helen did this with considerable velocity, then stopped to fix Carol with a stare that clearly indicated that she felt she had wasted quite enough time and had better things to do.

Carol said, "Last May I presume you spoke to Sally-Jean Cross about appearing on the program?"

For the first time Helen moved uneasily in her chair. "I do all the preparatory work before Madeline gets involved. It was just the early stages when she was . . ."

"Murdered by a person who may well have spoken to you last night."

An unreadable expression flickered across Helen's face but she gave no other response.

Carol said, "And this preparatory work took place after Ms. Cross had very publicly ended her relationship with Wilbur Shearing . . . who just happens to own this television station?"

Madeline interposed. "Carol, I have complete

37

autonomy on my show. The fact that Sally-Jean might say something embarrassing about Wilbur was secondary to whether she would be of interest to my viewers, and frankly, she was very newsworthy at the time."

Carol asked Helen a few more questions then let her go. When her rapid walk had taken her out of the room and the door had closed behind her expeditious back, Madeline chuckled. "I try to slow her down, too," she said, "but I've found it has no effect. Helen does everything at an unnerving pace . . . but she's efficient and loyal. I'd be lost without her."

"Has she been with you for long?"

"Helen? From the first." Adding with a tone of self-mockery, "And long before I was a household name."

She handed Carol a videotape. "And I can be as efficient as Helen at times. This is a video of my program last night . . . don't know if you caught it . . ." Carol shook her head. "Well, our feature item was a criminal psychiatrist discussing the mind of a serial murderer. Thought you'd want to see it, since it sparked this call."

"Can you remember what the caller said to you?"

"Possibly not exactly, but I hope I'm going to impress you, Carol, when you learn I take notes of all my telephone calls."

Momentarily irritated by Madeline Shipley's careful use of "Carol," intended, she was sure, to reinforce the impression of candor and friendship, she said shortly, "You can take it I'm impressed. So, referring to your notes, what can you tell me?"

Madeline smiled at her. "Would you feel more comfortable if I called you Inspector, rather than Carol?"

She was momentarily taken aback at Madeline's gentle derision. Ignoring the question, she said, "Please try to write down your conversation, word for word."

She watched Madeline concentrating on her notes, writing a few words, considering them. Madelilne caught her glance and grinned at her. "This is a bit of a blow to my pride. Helen's transcript is no doubt totally accurate, but I have to admit I'm having trouble."

"Try it out on me."

"Do you want a dramatic reading?"

Forced to smile, Carol said, "Not this first time."

Frowning over the sheet of paper, Madeline read: "Is that Madeline Shipley? (I said yes) You *are* Madeline Shipley, are you? How can I be sure? Say something more to me. (I said, What do you want me to say?) All right, that's enough. I know your voice. You think you've got power, don't you . . . but you've got responsibility too. Why did you put that doctor on your program? Do you think he could possibly know why they had to die? He doesn't. You don't. You're unfair and you're biased. (I said, In what way am I biased?) I'm not cruel. I don't want to hurt people, but they make me do it. (I said, are you claiming to be the Orange Strangler?) I'm not claiming to be. I *am*.'"

Madeline paused, looking up from the paper. "That's fairly close to what he said. Then, after I asked him how I could be sure he was the Orange Strangler he said: 'Oh, I'm the one. I'll prove it. Ask the police about the thumbs. Did you get that? Thumbs. I'll call back when you've done that.' "

"Thumbs — are you sure that was the word?"

"Absolutely. Are you going to tell me why he'd say that? What have thumbs got to do with it?"

Mark Bourke had made sure the information that each victim's thumbs and toes were tied with orange cord had been withheld from reporters and omitted from official reports. Although the fact of the feet being tied together had eventually leaked because shock had not completely blinded every person involved in discovering the naked bodies, the tying of the hands had never been mentioned.

Carol was always cautious with information she gave to media outlets, no matter how charming they might be. She said, "This mention of thumbs, if that *is* the word he used, may not be significant at all."

Madeline smiled at her. "So I have to ferret out why thumbs are significant myself, do I?"

"I'd appreciate it if you didn't mention it at all. Did you say anything afterwards to anyone about thumbs?"

"I suppose I did. It was such an odd thing to say and I wasn't aware it was a state secret at the time."

"Fair enough," said Carol. "Was that the last thing he said to you?"

"Almost. He was impossibly polite, if he was a murderer. He said goodbye very correctly."

"I've known murderers," Carol remarked sardonically, "whose manners were impeccable."

40

Madeline beamed at her. "What a line. Carol, you must come on my program!"

Chapter 4

Ignoring the crowd around her, Sybil leaned
against the low brick fence enclosing a dusty front
garden and glared at the yellow Day Ten call sheet.
DEATH DOWN UNDER was its confident heading,
followed rather quellingly by the names and
telephone numbers of the nearest hospital, fire,
ambulance and police services. Below these details
were the times and locations for Make-Up Call,
Wardrobe Call and Crew Call and then a grid setting
out various details including the scene number, the
estimated screen time it would take, the setting,

actors required, and exactly when and where everyone should be available.

Sybil was expected to arrive at Crew Call and be ready to teach her two charges whenever one or both were not in front of the cameras. Her short experience with movie-making had shown her that call sheets were notoriously optimistic when it came to scheduling scenes and estimating times, so she found it almost impossible to construct a firm timetable for herself and her students.

She flipped over to the second sheet, which listed essential props, transport of actors (status was implied by the type provided — for example, star Ripley Patterson naturally had a chauffeur and limousine), parking, additional equipment required, and the item which never failed to excite interest, when and where catering would supply the main meals.

She remembered Alice Fleming's words on her first day on the set: "A happy crew's a well-fed crew. Mark my words, dear, if the tucker's good, it'll be plain sailing. If not, well . . ." She had rolled her eyes heavenward to indicate the unfortunate consequences of such neglect.

A voice interrupted Sybil's somewhat jaundiced study of the call sheet. "Did you get to see yourself on yesterday's rushes?"

She looked up to meet Luke West's conspiratorial grin. Two days before there had been a crowd scene and he had persuaded her to join the extras with the comment that she might as well see herself on the screen in the finished movie provided she was lucky enough to escape the editor's scissors. At the end of each day's shooting all the film developed from the day before was screened for the director and camera operators in its rough uncut form and anyone in the crew was welcome to go to the studio at Darlinghurst to watch it. She had joined the crush in the viewing room a couple of times and had been fascinated by the way a scene she had watched through the tedium of its creation actually appeared on the screen. Most were not only filmed several times, but also from different angles and degrees of closeness.

Interesting though the rushes could be, if there was any possibility that Carol would be home, she gladly missed them. "I didn't see the rushes yesterday. Was I really up there on the screen?"

Luke patted her shoulder. "Ah, you're a natural, Syb. You positively glowed. Well-lit, too."

She grinned at that comment. Luke was the gaffer in charge of lighting each shot. She was already using film jargon confidently, and terms like rushes, gaffer, grip, clapper loader and boom swinger had slipped easily into her conversation.

Luke was about her height, lightly built, with thinning fair hair and quick, neat movements. He was unremittingly pleasant and his laconic, easy-going manner and apparent lack of hard-line opinions on any subject made it difficult for even the most determined antagonist to turn him into an opponent. Together with his assistant, Mick, whose official title was, rather fetchingly, Best Boy, Luke seemed to spend hours in deep discussion with the camera operator and the director regarding exactly how and where shadows should fall, highlights should occur and backlighting be used.

Before joining the crew, she hadn't realized that outside scenes were often artificially lit, either with

44

floodlamps or by means of hand-held reflectors out of the camera's field of vision. Now she found herself aware of the interplay of shadow and light in a way she had never been before.

Luke leaned companionably against the brick fence with her, saying, "Hope Vic gets a move on before the light changes again."

In script form the scene being shot seemed simple enough. The two young people, Kirra and Malcolm, were required to come out of a tired little Glebe house and into a neglected front garden. They were then to look over the fence into the street and see a sinister-looking man, played by a well-known Australian actor who had built his entire career on his ability to look balefully menacing. At this foreboding sight, each was required to react differently — Kirra with alarm, Malcolm with belligerence.

Sybil felt that if she were the director she could commit the whole scene to film in a few minutes, but Vic Carbond was his usual meticulous, morose self, complaining in his unpleasant nasal voice that the spectacle frames the character was wearing were casting unacceptable shadows on the actor's face and ruining the close-ups.

As director, Vic Carbond was treated by the crew with respect and instant obedience, but Sybil had heard muted comments about the difficulty of working with him, and some highly libelous remarks from Alice Fleming about his personal life and career. ("Likes a bit of rough stuff, you know, dear. Bondage and whips. Rumor has it there's been some people hurt around Vic . . . and you know about his X-rated videos, films, of course . . .")

45

Sybil looked at his gloomy, discontented expression and lank greasy hair, wondering who, if anyone, could want his company on a personal level.

Typically, Luke had been unruffled by Vic's irritable complaints, patiently experimenting with reflectors and lights until the offending shadows were removed. Vic's fussiness meant constant readjustment of the reflectors because the sun was moving inexorably and so changing the angle of light.

Sybil had been told to wait to one side to take charge of her students as they finished on camera, but the shooting stretched on and on. The call sheet had indicated the second scene of the day would last thirty seconds on the screen; so far an hour had been spent setting it up and another one attempting to shoot it to the director's satisfaction. The clapper loader changed the take number on the clapper board, the sound recordist called "Mark!", the boom operator positioned the microphone: another take began.

"Cut!" exclaimed Amy, one of the two assistant directors, after a muttered command from Vic Carbond. He looked at his watch with surly resignation. "Lunch," he said without enthusiasm.

"Lunch!" repeated Amy obediently. She was a short, rather stubby woman with a shock of bright orange hair, trendily ancient denim clothes and a wide grin. The distinct gap between her top front teeth often added a sibilant embellishment to her commands.

"I'll look after the kids," she said to Sybil, "Vic wants me to brief them on their next scene while they eat lunch. Okay?"

Sybil joined the stream of people heading to the

trestle tables set up beside the gray hulk of the catering truck, which had been parked at a rakish angle with the film unit's usual disregard for the letter of the law. Massy and Bruce, the caterers, stood with pride behind their culinary efforts. All main meals consisted of generous helpings of hot food, with a choice of meat dishes and a wide range of vegetables and salads. Desserts were always provided and it was hard for Sybil to see why everyone associated with the film industry didn't have a severe weight problem.

As Sybil lined up to collect a plate, Alice Fleming dug her in the ribs. "Syb, look — there's Wilbur Shearing. Vic better look out . . . he likes to keep a close eye on his investments."

Alice was pointing to a short, powerful figure in a dark suit who was immediately recognizable to most people because of his relentlessly persistent publicity machine. Not only did he appear regularly on his own television channel and in his own newspaper, but his business exploits assured him of coverage, not always favorable, in opposition media outlets as well.

"They say," said Alice breathlessly, "he just never got over her murder. I mean that girlfriend of his, Sally-Jean."

"Rubbish," said Luke, who was standing behind them in the line. "Shearing'd already dumped her when she got herself killed."

Alice viewed this contradiction with disdain. "You're just repeating what you heard. I knew her personally. I can tell you things were a lot different to the way they seemed."

Luke was disinclined to follow up her comments,

so she contented herself with an emphatic nod and turned her attention to lunch. Her appetite for food as well as gossip was healthy and she began to shovel food onto her plate with industry as she exclaimed, "You see he's done it again — the Orange Strangler! In the paper this morning they say he might be dressing as a woman, just to lure them to their deaths!" Before either could respond, she continued with almost breathless gusto, "Dreadful, isn't it, killing girls that way. Why do you think he does it?"

Shrugging, Luke said, "He's a psycho, I suppose."

Although she had previously given it no thought, Sybil surprised herself by saying, "How do you know it's a man? There's been no mention of rape."

Both looked at her with surprise, Alice even halting her food collection to say scornfully, "Of course it's a man, dear. Women just don't go round doing things like that."

Luke was frowning. "Why would any woman set out to kill a string of other women?"

"Why would a man?" asked Sybil.

Alice hooted derision. "Why would a man? Oh, honestly, Syb, you know the answer yourself. I bet he's some little squirt who can't get a girl of his own. It's revenge. Just typical of a man to take it out on a woman. They all do it, you know, one way or the other."

Luke had regained his good humor. "Don't be so hard on us men," he said, laughing as he put his arm around Alice's waist.

"You're all alike," she said playfully, but Sybil felt the underlying hardness in her remark.

She watched Luke and Alice continue to spar with their customary good-natured antagonism, thinking that with Alice Fleming there was no mystery because you saw what you got — a gossip who was superficial but entertaining. Luke perhaps was different. She wondered what was really there, hidden behind his pleasant, easy-going exterior. She grinned to herself. Probably a pleasant, easy-going interior.

Alice Fleming had given Sybil her assessment of Luke West within the first few days. "Bit of a poofter, dear," she had said. "Probably because he was brought up in an all-female household. Not really natural, is it . . . specially for a young boy. He's not married, nor likely to be. Bit of a loner, but awfully nice to talk to. Wouldn't get my hopes up over him, though. He hasn't got much to offer someone like you."

Her thoughts were interrupted by Charlie Date, who was smiling ingratiatingly through his drooping mustache. Finding this affability rather more trying than his previous surliness, she said shortly, "Yes?"

"Amy says she'll need the kids for the next two hours, so you can take a breather. Wondered if you wanted to come with me . . . I've got to scout ahead for the next location . . ."

"Sorry," she said, "but I've a lesson I must prepare."

"Sure," he replied without expression.

She watched his bulk move through the crowd clustered around the trestle tables and tried to imagine him as a father with children, but somehow he didn't fit the role. He seemed more an isolated figure who was somehow out of sync with the rest of the world.

Bourke was restored to his tidy self. He favored clothing of beige and brown, and as he came into her office Carol wondered idly if someone had once told him those were his colors. Today he wore a brown-gray suit, and, as always, a white shirt and subdued tie. She was aware of a contradiction between his appearance and his manner. He dressed conservatively, yet his approach was usually full of relaxed humor and he was one of the few people in her working sphere who could tease her with impunity.

He dumped several manila folders on her desk. "Your commands, as always, followed to the letter, though I did hear there was the odd, but, of course, hushed complaint about our unreasonable demands. Anyway, here's the stuff on Alissa Harvey."

He sat down at her gesture, adding, "And I've got the techos onto the job of monitoring the calls to Madeline Shipley at the channel. Should be well set up before the show tonight. I've told them to make sure she understands she has to keep him talking as long as possible."

Carol leaned back in her chair and sighed. "The call could be a dead end. Although the mention of thumbs is tantalizing, you know as well as I do there could have been a leak about that part of the m.o.

And even if he is the one, he might be far too sharp to call again, or if he does, he'll know to keep it to a few moments so there's not much chance of a trace."

"There's always voice prints."

"Fine, but not much use if we haven't got a suspect to match them with."

Bourke raised his eyebrows. "Wilbur Shearing?" he said.

Carol nodded. "Sure, it's worth a go if we ever get a recording. Both Madeline Shipley and her assistant, Helen Tolsten, said he spoke with an almost exaggerated Australian accent, as if disguising his usual voice."

"Not Australian?"

"They both thought he was an Aussie, but got the impression he was deliberately trying to sound broad Australian, because he usually has a more clipped accent."

Bourke looked gratified. "Shearing was educated in England, went to Oxford and all that." Adding derisively, "He hardly sounds Australian, he speaks so well."

Carol made a face at him. "You're keen to nail Wilbur Shearing because you haven't got anyone else in mind. He's got alibis, Mark. He looks clean."

"I don't like him. He's an arrogant bastard." Bourke grinned. "Not, Carol, that *that* would influence me. Besides, he might be a little bit old for the psychiatrist's profile — psychopaths, as they always assure us, usually commit their most spectacular crimes when they're fairly young. Our Wilbur's pushing forty-five or so. Besides, to be fair to the man, he's paid off two wives and unloaded countless girlfriends, all apparently without feeling an overwhelming impulse to murder."

Carol began to play with a gold pen that Sybil had given her. "I gather our senior forensic psychiatrist has given his set interview again," she said.

"Yep. The usual stuff and the papers love printing it, especially as he looks like Sigmund Freud on a good day and always sounds like he knows what he's talking about."

"You don't think he does?"

"Sure he does, but he ignores the uncomfortable fact that some serial killers just refuse to fit the stereotype he's prepared for them. Anyway, he said with his usual fatherly authority that the Orange Strangler is a relatively young male possessing a lifelong personality disturbance with no sense of right or wrong. The good doctor thinks he's been brought up in some sort of strict religious household because of the way the bodies are laid out. He may hate and fear women, but this may not be apparent in his everyday behavior. He might have a record of anti-social behavior but he almost certainly projects a superficially charming and acceptable face to the world. You know the rest, and it's not much help. Probably above average in intelligence, might have a history of cruelty towards animals, but then again, might relate better to animals than people. When caught such a person is usually diagnosed as a psychopath, or, more trendily, a sociopath. Basically mad, bad and dangerous to know, but wrapped up in an attractive human package."

"Human package?" said Carol. "Mark, with such creativity you're wasted on the police force."

He smiled at her mockery. "And I'm non-sexist too. Considered the human package in question could be a woman?"

"It's not likely, is it — not with that modus operandi and female victims, but it would be stupid to rule it out entirely."

"Teamwork? Think of Ian Brady and Myra Hindley in the English Moors murders. What do you think of the idea of a man and woman working together?"

"That sort of combination almost always has some kind of sadistic sexual perversion as a unifying motive. The murders we're looking at here appear to be ritualistic sacrifices with no sexual violation of any kind."

Bourke shrugged. "Probably impotent, or sublimating his sexual drive into religious fantasy . . . how about giving black masses and satanism a run? See the paper this morning? There's an article about some nut who thinks she's called up the victims at a seance. Swears they told her devil-worshippers killed them."

"Great," said Carol. "Surprised someone hasn't come up with a theory involving ASIO or the CIA."

"Give them time, Carol, give them time. They will."

"Knowing you, Mark, you've got some sort of imaginative profile to describe the person we're looking for."

"I sure have. I'm positive he's male and working alone. Not sure about his age, but he's not a kid.

He's not a rapist and if he has a record it'll be for minor offenses. He's not stupid. He's getting to love the notoriety and thinks he's got us on the run. Has some sort of grudge against women in general, or perhaps specific women who upset him. It goes without saying that in some ways at least, he's psychopathic. He probably lives alone and has few, if any, real friends, although he may have many acquaintances who will all say when we get him: 'It can't be true! He's such a nice guy!' "

"He doesn't have to live alone, Mark. Remember the Yorkshire Ripper was married, and his wife didn't suspect him."

"Well, living alone or not, he's convincing in the role he's chosen to play. We know he drives a car. He may have something to do with sailing or water sports. He's neat and systematic. He's familiar with Sydney, although possibly not the western areas of the city. My feeling is he was brought up in a religious household, possibly dominated by his mother . . . Don't raise your eyebrows, Carol, I'm not criticizing a matriarchal upbringing."

She gestured for him to continue.

"It's fairly obvious he persuades his victims to accompany him without too much difficulty — they go unsuspecting to their deaths. This indicates he's not threatening or strange enough to alarm them. In fact, I'd bet he's extremely pleasant and easy to get on with. He doesn't use alcohol or drugs to stun them, but takes them by surprise from behind. He's reasonably strong, since he has to move the inert weight of the body to another location, undress it and arrange it to his satisfaction. About that he's obsessive."

Carol didn't attempt to remove the doubt from her voice. "If I understand you, you think this obsession comes from a matriarchal, but religious, upbringing?"

With a grin, Bourke said, "It's *my* imagination, Carol, and you did ask. Anyway, you can hardly deny that our boy is rather kinky about religion."

Carol wrote the word "orange," drew a circle around it and idly began to list associated words. She said, "I think in some way he sees these women as sacrifices."

"To what god? And what's the point of the ritual?"

"Why orange?" said Carol, looking at the words she'd listed: fruit, sun, tangerine, gold, brass, copper, carroty, gingery, golden, amber.

Bourke groaned. "Why orange, indeed? I had the bright idea it might have something to do with the Orange People . . . that eastern cult thing . . . but it was a dead end. Then we got a psychologist to come up with reasons why orange might be significant. She went round in circles and we went with her. Almost convinced me our murderer was indulging in word games with us and so using orange cord because of the play on words between gilt meaning golden and guilt meaning I-did-it. Then I came to my senses and ditched the whole idea."

"Maybe he just likes the color."

Bourke was looking disgruntled. "Maybe he just happened to have a supply of that particular rope. For all we know it could have been purple, or blue or green, and we'd be sitting here trying to read some significance into one of those colors instead."

"Why does he make it so easy for us to identify

the bodies by leaving all the clothes and personal effects at the scene?"

Bourke considered the question. "Well," he said, "why carry away something that could incriminate you?"

"Or," said Carol, leaning forward, "perhaps the identity of the person is important to his purpose, only we haven't tumbled to the link. That's why he's ringing Madeline Shipley, because we haven't publicized what he wants publicized."

"Could be."

Carol said, "Think the call to Madeline Shipley is genuine?"

Bourke was cheerful again. "Good chance it is. And I'm sure he'll follow it up, and that could just be his big mistake. He loves the attention, the publicity. He's getting very confident, taking risks, especially with the time it takes to lay the bodies out. And, of course, he has grounds for pride — he's getting better at murder. No more scratches from his victims as he strangles them."

"He's been efficient from the first, Mark. After all, we haven't caught him, have we?"

His voice determined, Bourke said, "Not yet, but nailing him will be a delight."

She managed to repress the bitter comment that there would almost certainly be another victim before an arrest was achieved and asked Bourke to summarize the findings on Alissa Harvey.

She knew Bourke would systematically tick off the main points with unerring accuracy. She valued his opinions and admired his abilities. He disarmed with his flippant remarks and casual manner, but underneath was a keen mind, a talent for observation

56

and a tenacious streak that made him a formidable detective.

She didn't interrupt, continuing her aimless drawing of arrows and circles while she listened. Alissa Harvey's body had been positively identified by her parents. Bourke himself had interviewed them, but they were so distressed he had decided to leave detailed questioning for a day or so. The victim had just turned twenty-two and had been a talented free-lance photographer. She had been last seen at four-thirty in the offices of a magazine for which she regularly worked. No one had come forward to say where she had been from that point onwards, although Bourke had arranged for her photograph to be printed in the press and shown on television.

Alissa Harvey had consumed coffee and biscuits an hour or so before she died. She had been strangled with orange cord in the same way as the other victims, dying somewhere between seven-thirty and nine-thirty the evening before her body was found. Her murderer had left no signs of his or her presence — no blood, no skin traces or clothing fibers. The victim had not been sexually assaulted. As in the other two cases, lividity indicated she had been killed at one place and her body moved and arranged in the disused factory yard where she was found. Her belongings were neatly placed beside her feet, including an expensive compact camera, her wallet and money. Nothing appeared to be missing. Alissa Harvey's fingerprints, along with other smudged and unidentifiable ones, were found on the leather surfaces. Bourke added, "The lab used the latest laser stuff to sight the prints, but no go. Anyway, our boy's far too smart to leave a print around."

Carol wanted to know about the film in the camera. Bourke handed her the developed prints. "I've given Ferguson a copy of each one and he's tracking them down."

As she shuffled through the photographs he added casually, "Could be interesting that there's a photo of Madeline Shipley there." He pointed it out, adding, "Think it's taken on the set of her program. Interesting link, eh?"

"May I keep these prints?"

Bourke nodded. "Sure, had several sets made."

"And I want Ferguson's report as soon as possible."

Bourke nodded assent, then went on to discuss the forensic report on the crime scene. Close examination of the abandoned factory yard had revealed a confusion of footprints in the mud and a clear tire print near the gate. The tire was a popular and reasonably cheap mass-produced steel radial and had no outstanding wear patterns. The footprints were indistinct and some obviously belonged to the two elderly street men who had discovered the body. When they had raised the alarm a crowd had gathered before police could arrive and cordon off the area, so there was also a multitude of footprints made by curious onlookers.

"It's all pretty hopeless as far as distinct shoe prints are concerned," he said, "but even so, even with all the shuffling around, I don't think the crowd would have completely obliterated any marks indicating the body was dragged across the yard."

"Is this your indirect way of saying it wasn't dragged?"

"I'm saying," said Bourke, "she was carried, and

that makes it more likely to be a man — Alissa Harvey wasn't fat, but she was a reasonable size, and, I think, too heavy for a woman to carry easily, especially since she was a dead weight, so to speak."

"But not impossible."

"Never impossible," he said, adding deadpan, "Surely you know I'd be the last person to underestimate the power of a woman."

Chapter 5

Sybil said, "I didn't complain when you insisted we watch tonight's edition of *The Shipley Report* while we ate the meal I slaved to produce, but to follow it with a videotape of last night's show is going a bit far." She added, teasing, "I trust your interest in Madeline Shipley is purely professional?"

"Purely — though she's a knockout in person."

Sybil looked at the screen where Madeline was doing the introduction to her last night's show. As her face was replaced by the first of a series of ads, Sybil said, "She looks pretty good on camera too,

Carol. You know she's married to some artist, don't you . . . happily married, I believe."

Carol grinned at her tone. "Darling, it's your little red-headed self I love and no one else. Stunning though Madeline Shipley may be, she can never tempt me from your side."

Sybil was curious. "What's she like? It's hard to believe she's as nice as she appears. I keep feeling it must be an act."

"I don't know if she's genuine or not. She makes a good job of seeming to be. However, the most important thing is that she just might be a point of contact with the serial killer. Otherwise, we're just as far away as we were when the first murder happened."

"Surprising she didn't mention anything about the call on the show tonight. An announcement like that would cream the opposition."

Carol nodded. "Impressed me too. I asked her not to mention it, but there must have been a huge temptation to announce the Orange Strangler was calling her direct, particularly since she and Pierre Brand are locked in a ratings war in that time slot."

"So she *is* as nice as she appears," said Sybil with a note of mockery.

"Maybe. Or perhaps she's going for something more, like a personal interview with a serial killer. That would be worth holding your fire for."

"Cynic," said Sybil.

"Just realistic. Madeline Shipley's a professional, and getting the best audience share is the name of the game."

"In his program last night Pierre Brand took his usual low-key, responsible approach to the stranglings, then offered to act as a go-between for any person who might come forward after watching his show. Said he'd smooth the way for anyone who realized they had a serial murderer in the family. It was a heartfelt plea, no doubt prompted by Pierre's desire to serve his public."

Carol smiled wryly at her scathing tone. In the past Sybil had had every reason to dislike Brand and his particular approach to news stories.

She said, "Madeline's no Pierre Brand. She struck me as reasonable and fair, though I could be sucked in, of course. And whether she's a smiling monster or the nicest human being yet created is quite irrelevant, since I've got to be friendly no matter what . . . she's our best bet yet of getting to this killer."

Fast-forwarding through the rest of the advertisements, Carol clicked on Madeline as she began to speak with her usual polished, charming sincerity: "Tonight we have as our guest Dr. Daniel Dunn, noted criminal psychiatrist who has specialized in analyzing the psychopathic mind. Dr. Dunn has been involved in some of the most infamous cases in Australia's crime history and is well-qualified to speak on the Orange Strangler . . ."

Carol watched the program closely, taking notes and several times stopping the tape to run back over part of the interview. Then she said to Sybil, "Imagine you're the murderer, and you've just viewed that program. What would make you pick up a phone and ring Madeline Shipley?"

"I don't know — maybe that I wanted to give my side of the story. I assume he's got some motive that makes sense to him, even if it mightn't to us."

"The trouble is, we haven't really got a clue what that motive is."

"Carol, what could make someone want to kill four young women that way? It's not sex, is it?"

Carol sighed. "Certainly they're not raped — there's no oral or vaginal intercourse or, for that matter, any semen on the body or clothes." She grimaced. "Some attackers ejaculate over their victims or some item of clothing, but there's nothing like that here."

Shaking her head, Sybil said, "Why are so many women attacked? Why are there so many rapes? And not just individual rapes, but pack rapes. It can't be lack of sexual availability — we're not living in the Victorian ages, for God's sake!"

"It's power, it isn't sex. Rape's just the ultimate way to express dominance. And it isn't just women who are raped. Men rape men far more often than you'd realize, and —"

She broke off as the telephone rang. "Carol Ashton . . . Yes, Mark . . . yes, get onto it. You know what to do. I'll be in early tomorrow morning."

Replacing the receiver she responded to Sybil's interrogative look, "Our possible strangler has called again, but not the television station and not the phone we were monitoring. He telephoned and left a message with Madeline Shipley's husband. And it's an unlisted number. Now isn't that interesting?"

The night was still, steeped in moonlight, warm with promise. A possum hissed asthmatically in the

63

gum tree outside the bedroom window. Carol groaned, shivered, as Sybil arched beneath her, her thigh between Carol's legs, heart beating against Carol's heart, skin slippery with sweat sliding beneath Carol's fingers.

Carol's mouth was seeking reassurance in the taste of her, tongue thrusting and seeking, intoxicated by sensation. Riding a tide, dizzy with the growing intensity of desire, the thrilling irritation becoming a delightful pain.

Carol heard herself speak. "Darling," she said. She examined the word, turning it over in the torrent of feeling to see its shape.

Sybil moved under her until she could take a nipple in her mouth, sliding her tongue in circles, sucking, teasing. Carol couldn't think any more. Everything was receding into a roaring void of color and sound. She stiffened, not wanting it yet, determined to wait until the burning ache consumed her completely, until every thought was burned away.

She began to count silently to herself, willing her eager body to postpone the passionate release it craved, but Sybil's hand was between her legs, stroking, urgent, driving her insistently towards the point where she could not avoid bursting into release.

Conscious only of the need to stay submerged in quivering sensation, free from anything but feeling, she wailed with almost reluctant ecstasy as her orgasm began.

Began and continued, wave upon wave, shaking her almost unconscious with its force, exhausting her until she felt she could barely breathe.

Sybil was cradling her, whispering to her. She

tried to listen to the words, but they blurred and faded as she slipped into sleep.

Chapter 6

"Tell me."

Bourke raised an eyebrow. "Well, Carol, it's a puzzle, unless perhaps the famous Orange Strangler is a personal friend of Madeline Shipley and her husband, Paul Crusoe. The unlisted number, La Shipley tells me, is only given to a select few. This could be a breakthrough."

Unconvinced, Carol said, "Could be, but I can't imagine he'd be so stupid as to narrow the field this way. He must know we haven't got even close to him, so why make it easier for us?"

"How about the good old Catch-Me-Before-I-Kill-Again scenario?"

"A creative thought, Mark, but I don't think so. I have a strong feeling he means it as a red herring."

"What if there *was* no call? What if it's Shipley's painter husband?"

Carol frowned as she brushed a piece of lint from the skirt of her severe blue suit. "Paul Crusoe . . . wasn't there some fuss in the art world about him?"

"You must mean the time he crucified a chicken."

"What? You're kidding me."

Grinning at her reaction, Bourke said, "The unfortunate chicken was already dead, Carol, otherwise the RSPCA would have been involved, not that Paul Crusoe would have minded — he engineered the whole thing to gain as much notoriety as possible. I rang a friend at the Art Gallery of New South Wales to ask about Shipley's husband and she reminded me of the whole scandal."

Carol was tempted to ask if he had an interest in art, again aware that, although she knew every aspect of his professional life, she had very little idea of his interests outside the police force.

Almost as though he sensed her thoughts, he said, "We went to school together — years ago, of course — but we've kept in touch, so Pat was happy to give me the behind-the-scenes story. Every year, along with the big art competitions like the Archibald Prize, there are several smaller ones with quite substantial budgets — for example the Rickard Prize for Religious Art. Two years ago Paul Crusoe entered a so-called work of art entitled *Christ Transmogrified*. It consisted of a perfectly traditional painting of the crucifixion, except that in place of Christ's body he

67

had affixed a dead chicken, wings outstretched, feathers and all."

Smiling at the bizarre image this conjured up, she said, "Well, why the fuss? They could have told him it was a joke and refused to show it."

His grin widened. "The trustees were thrown into a complete tizzy, but after furious secret discussions, it was arranged for the Health Department to step in and declare the entry a threat to public health. *Christ Transmogrified* was then withdrawn, but not before Paul Crusoe's name had had a real airing."

"So Paul Crusoe might do anything for publicity?"

"I get that impression, and he seems to need all the help he can get. Pat tells me he's an also-ran as an artist — most of the interest he generates is because of his wife's success. And Pat says it's generally thought that Madeline Shipley not only supports Paul Crusoe, but she also pays private galleries substantial sums to mount his exhibitions. In short, she's his meal ticket."

Carol rubbed her jaw thoughtfully. "Any kind of sensational publicity would help both of them. How about this: Madeline gets the idea from a crank call she claims is genuine, and with her husband's help, she follows it up with a second call, knowing full well we haven't bugged his unlisted number."

"Tsk," said Bourke. "Next you'll be saying Madeline Shipley herself is the killer."

Carol smiled at him. "She can't be. I've checked. In all but one of the murders she was on the air or tied up at the crucial times with the preparation of programs."

Bourke was grinning. "You don't trust anyone, do you?"

"No," said Carol promptly, then frowned. Why had she said that without thought? She trusted Mark Bourke professionally . . . and Sybil . . . In her private life didn't she trust Sybil?

"This is boring," said Malcolm Murtry, glaring balefully at the open textbook.

Limited though Sybil considered Malcolm's acting talents to be, she felt some admiration for his mastery of sulky truculence. He was broodingly handsome in an undeveloped teenage way, and, she strongly suspected, rather stupid.

"Life does contain some boring moments," she observed, "no doubt put there to balance the truly exciting ones."

He glanced sideways at her, but she kept her expression neutral. He said, "Kirra doesn't have to do this. Why do I?"

"She's in a scene at the moment. She'll have her turn in here after lunch while you're out shooting."

"Should be learning my lines. This is just a waste of time."

How true, thought Sybil. "The exercise is straightforward, Malcolm, if you read the instructions at the top. Let me help you get started."

He sighed, mumbled to himself and eventually began to scribble desultory words on his writing pad. Sybil had found that his concentration rarely lasted more than five minutes, so she was not surprised when he laid down his pen, stretched as though surfacing from hours of hard mental work, and started a diversionary tactic, one dear to many students, the conversation with the teacher.

"Sybil," he said cheerfully, "you know the Orange Strangler, the guy who's killing those girls, well, I knew one of them."

Despite herself, Sybil was interested. "She was a friend of yours?"

He gave a charming, self-deprecating smile. "Not exactly. That first one, Maria Kelly, she was an actor, you know. Well, I was in something with her, just before she was bumped off. Creepy, eh? It was one of my first parts on television. Kept a tape of it, if you'd like to see it. It was a year ago and I was just getting somewhere, you know."

His enthusiasm mounted as he embarked upon his favorite subject, himself. "You see, you need exposure, and this was a great break for me. Short, mind you, and I didn't have much to say. But I made an impact."

"I'm sure you did," Sybil said without conviction. "And Maria Kelly, what part did she have? It was an ad, was it?"

"Oh, no. I'd done ads before, of course. A lot of them, actually. Got tapes of them, too. But this time it was a re-enactment of a crime, see. You know the sort of thing, where you play out the murderer and the victims and all that. Know what I mean?"

"What was the crime?"

"Jeez, can't remember after all this time, but the important thing for me was it gave me exposure.

You've got to get your face known . . . You remember seeing me anytime?"

"Must have missed you," said Sybil with artificial regret.

"Pity," said Malcolm, "I'm real good."

Malcolm had been summoned to wardrobe and Kirra was still filming, so Sybil got herself a mug of coffee, put her feet up and contemplated nothing in particular.

"Can I come in?"

She looked up at Luke West's smiling face. "Sure, but it's hot in the caravan."

He settled himself opposite her, arranging his wiry body neatly along the bench seat. "I don't mind the heat, and Vic doesn't need me for the moment. Besides the pleasure of your company, I have to admit I'm hiding from Alice."

Politeness made her look questioning. He responded immediately. "She reminds me of my ex-wife, you see. Always wanting to tell me what to do."

"I didn't know you'd been married."

"No? Why would you?"

Thinking of Alice's gossipy references to Luke as being homosexual, she said vaguely, "Must have been something someone said . . ."

Luke was amused. "Don't believe everything Alice puts out. She is, to put it mildly, often careless with the truth."

He smoothed his fair hair with quick precise

71

movements. "Can't help noticing Charlie Date's got some interest in you . . . It's none of my business, but he can be a bit odd . . ."

He stood. "The fact is, I don't think Charlie really likes women all that much." He made a face at her frown. "Starting to sound like Alice, aren't I?"

Before she could reply he had waved a farewell and stepped quickly out of the cramped caravan. Sybil heard Vic Carbond's unpleasant nasal voice, Luke's lighter tones, and then Vic clambered in to smile at her.

She had noticed that most of Vic Carbond's infrequent smiles were short-lived, and this one was no exception. He slumped on the bench Luke had just vacated and stared morosely at her. He was wearing grubby jeans and a startlingly white T-shirt emblazoned with DEATH DOWN UNDER in vermilion.

"They've just come," he said, shoving a flat packet across the table. "Should have been here day one, but now we've got them, I want the whole crew wearing them."

The packet contained two T-shirts, each bearing the title of the film, but one on a background of pale green and the other an eggshell blue.

"Guessed your size," said Vic, smiling again. "And thought those ones would go with your red hair."

Sybil was not surprised to notice that his teeth were discolored. While she was wondering why he, as director, had stooped to delivering T-shirts to her, Vic gave her the answer.

"Actually," he said, "I wanted a word with you in private. It's all to do with the Education Department. Last film when I had kids in the cast there were

72

some complaints about the education they were getting. I don't have to tell you it's pretty hopeless trying to give them proper teaching on the set, but the important thing is to make it look good. Everything to do with kids has got to look aboveboard, know what I mean?"

Sybil was amused at his anxiety until she remembered an ugly rumor Alice had delighted in repeating. Word was, Alice had said, that young boys cast in one of Vic's recent movies had been involved in extra-curricular filming for the pederast market.

She said, "I don't think you need worry, Vic. I've kept detailed records and I've been in touch with Malcolm and Kirra's schools. I'm sure everything will check out."

Rising, he patted her shoulder. "Want you to know I've been keeping an eye on you, Sybil. You're doing a good job. I'd be glad to put a word in for you if you want another position as tutor."

She nodded, resisting the impulse to shrink away from his touch. She wondered how many people were willing to put up with Vic Carbond's attentions for the advantage of what he might do for them.

Mark Bourke waved at the whiteboard that took up one wall of his office. "There just isn't a link, Carol — not one I can see, anyway."

She concentrated on the grid of lines and words, letting her eyes wander, looking for any pattern that might emerge.

Each victim's life and death was detailed in columns of Bourke's neat printing. Maria Kelly, twenty-three, bit-part actor, dark hair, brown eyes, found strangled last December at Audley Weir picnic grounds in the Royal National Park to the south of Sydney. Sally-Jean Cross, twenty-eight, journalist, bleached blonde hair, hazel eyes, her body found at Manly Dam Reserve not far from where Carol lived. Narelle Dent, thirty-three, supermarket check-out operator, tinted auburn hair and blue eyes, discovered off the road near picnic benches in Galston Gorge to the northeast of the city. Alissa Harvey, twenty-two, photographer, brown hair and brown eyes, found lying in the yard of a disused factory at Alexandria, an old suburb just to the south of central Sydney.

Bourke had noted in red: *Why no body in the Western Suburbs? Unfamiliar with the area, or does he live there?*

Carol said, "They didn't know each other, come from the same area, go to the same school or share an interest of any kind?"

"Nope. Nor is there any common physical characteristic — Alissa Harvey was a big, healthy girl, Sally-Jean and the first victim, Maria Kelly, were fashionably skinny and Narelle was average in every way."

"She was the only one married?"

"Yes, Carol, but divorced. The press tried to beat up a story about suburban orgies — partner-swapping and the usual stuff, men with men and women with women and then all in with everyone else, but eventually it petered out."

"What was the source?"

"Of the stories? A gossip, big-noting to a reporter. You know how it is . . . loving the attention, so

74

embroidering the truth until it becomes a pack of lies."

Carol remembered that the headlines after Narelle Dent's death in August had been concerned not only with the fact that she was the Orange Strangler's third victim, but with the idea that she was promiscuous and a "bad mother" who, it was implied, had somehow brought her fate upon herself.

"What about the ex-husband," she said.

"No particular animosity there. The only unusual thing about the divorce was that she gave up custody of her daughter without a whimper. Might call her an unnatural mother." A shade of concern suddenly crossed his face. He said hastily, "I'm sure she had her reasons . . ." Carol looked at him steadily, knowing he was thinking of how she had given up her son.

She thought, But not without a whimper, Mark.

He broke the uncomfortable silence. "I've followed up religious beliefs because of the way the bodies were laid out. Hoped there would be some link, say that they all had something to do with some way-out belief, but it was no go. However, in a negative way there *is* a pattern, almost as if he decided to wipe out a member of each major religion. For example, Maria Kelly was, as her name might suggest, a Catholic, but not a particularly strict one. Then you have Sally-Jean Cross from a Jewish family, Narelle Dent whose parents are humanists and made sure she was brought up an atheist, or, at worst, an agnostic — and lastly Alissa, who had a fundamentalist fire-and-brimstone upbringing."

He grinned as he added, "And I expect my theory

will be proved when the next victim is a Muslim or a Buddhist. What do you think?"

Carol was staring meditatively at the whiteboard. "I think," she said, "that they were all killed on weeknights. No one on the weekend. Why would that be?"

Bourke ran his finger down the list. "We noticed that, but it's probably just by chance. The first was on a Thursday, the second Wednesday, third another Thursday and Alissa Harvey last Tuesday night. Think he's got a weekend job?"

"Could be coincidence, of course. It's hardly a big enough sample to be sure there's a pattern."

Bourke rubbed his chin. "How about this: he works his way into being a casual acquaintance with each one, but it's not the sort of relationship a girl would waste a weekend date on, so he asks them for coffee or a drink during the week, when they're more likely to accept."

"That sounds good," said Carol, "and it could be true. Or, of course, it might be as simple as the fact those are the only times he has access to a car, or time off from a night-shift, or the moon's full . . ."

"Checked that," said Bourke, "but no recurrence of full moons." His voice became mournful. "And I did live in hopes . . . you know how I love 'Lunar Madness Baffles Cops' headlines."

Madeline Shipley's husband looked as though he had put considerable work into looking the part of an artist. There was a faint aroma of oil paint, turpentine and varnish about him. His mousy straight hair was longish, his dark eyes serious, his thin fingers bearing traces of paint. The battered pair of military trousers and matching khaki shirt blotched here and there with oil colors hung loosely on his gaunt frame. He took Carol's hand for a moment, exerted a slight pressure and released it slowly.

Carol was formal. "Mr. Crusoe, I'm very sorry to interrupt your work. I know you saw Detective Sergeant Bourke last night, but I'd be grateful if you could spare the time to discuss the call with me."

Crusoe drifted rather than walked as he made his way across his studio, saying in a slow soft voice that matched his movements, "Do call me Paul, Inspector, and I shall call you Carol. Madeline has told me all about you." He gestured vaguely. "Do find a seat . . . move anything that's in the way . . ."

The room was a chaos of easels, painting materials and canvases in various stages of completion. His painting seemed to rely upon the juxtapositioning of violent shades and distorted shapes — everywhere she looked hot clashing colors glared. He perched himself on a tall stool near an easel, watching with relaxed interest as Carol extracted a chair from a pile of canvases.

"Have you ever considered having your portrait painted?" he inquired.

"No, never."

He shook his head in slow regret. "You should. You have the personality. People think it's the bones, the face, but they're wrong. It's the inner self. But of course you would realize that."

She was cynical enough to decide that Paul Crusoe was trying to portray the two of them as soul mates to win her over. She said, "I don't want to waste your time, Paul, so perhaps we can discuss the call . . ."

"The call? Oh, yes. You must understand I have very little to do with Madeline's professional life. Our careers are quite separate, our goals quite different . . . That doesn't mean we have nothing in common . . . On the contrary . . ."

Carol thought, For God's sake get to the point! "The call?" she prompted.

Soon she couldn't decide if he was being deliberately obstructive or if his concentration was of the will-o'-the-wisp variety. Every time she thought she had pinned him down to the subject of the telephone call he slipped away.

She had expected to spend about half an hour with Paul Crusoe, but it took an hour of patient listening and questioning before she was satisfied she had everything he had to say. The phone had rung at seven-thirty last night, straight after Madeline's program — he always watched it — and a man's voice, speaking in a very broad Australian accent, had asked if he were Paul Crusoe. Assured that this was the case, he then announced that he was the Orange Strangler, going on to say he was sure Madeline would want to interview him now that she knew from the police he was genuine.

Paul Crusoe asked how he had got the unlisted number, but he ignored the question. Paul had then pointed out that he could still ring Madeline at the channel. This amused the caller, who said he didn't intend to make a call that could be traced. He went on with instructions. Paul Crusoe was to tell Madeline Shipley to prepare a program devoted entirely to his series of murders, but enough time was to be left for him to be personally interviewed. He refused to answer any questions from Paul, terminating the call with the words: "Tell her I'll contact her when the program's ready. And I'll be wanting it scheduled mid-week. Tell her that."

Carol had to work hard on Crusoe to extract the short list of people who knew the unlisted number.

He said, "And Madeline, of course. Madeline has the number. We speak every day, you know. She spends so much time at the channel, and I'm here, of course, working . . . It is important to communicate, to clearly communicate . . ."

Carol had to smile at that last remark. Clear communication and Paul Crusoe seemed mutually exclusive. "It is," she agreed, rising as Madeline came into the studio. She was wearing a cool flowing turquoise dress that swirled around her as she moved, making Carol feel over-severe in her tailored suit.

"Carol! You're not going? I've just asked Edna to prepare us all a light lunch."

Paul Crusoe sighed. "Madeline, I do wish you'd remember I don't like to eat lunch when I'm working. I'll get something later. You two go ahead without me."

Madeline laughed at him, getting a reluctant smile in return. "Paul," she said, "Edna's already told me what you've eaten this morning. How you stay so thin escapes me. It isn't work that keeps you from lunch, it's earlier gluttony." She gave him an affectionate half-hug, adding, "Carol and I will entertain ourselves. You go back to your daubing, darling."

She smiled at Carol. "So the thumbs were the clincher, eh? Your Mark Bourke explained it all to me. Means the calls really are genuine, I suppose."

Carol was cautious. "They could be, but it's dangerous to be totally convinced. A lot of investigations have gone off the rails because false evidence was taken to be reliable."

"I hope I'm not wasting your time, Carol."

"Of course you're not. Everything has to be followed up . . . and you will tell me if he contacts you some other way, won't you?"

"Why would you doubt it?" said Madeline, clearly affronted.

"He told your husband he wants you to make him a program and then interview him for it. If he means what he says, you could have every television set in Australia tuned in to your show."

"Look, Carol, I want this guy caught, just like everyone else does. You know I told the police the first time I heard from him and this time I did the same. So why are you suggesting I won't continue to cooperate?"

To pacify her indignation Carol said lightly, "Madeline, I'm just too suspicious. It might be my job . . ."

Madeline repeated her offer of lunch. Carol's protests about lack of time were smiled down. "Be as brief as you like, Carol. I know you're seeing Wilbur Shearing at three this afternoon."

"It's public knowledge?" said Carol, using her tone to indicate surprised displeasure.

"Not at all. Actually, Wilbur told me you had an appointment. He doesn't like the unexpected . . . Wanted to know what you were like." When Carol

80

said nothing, she continued, "I told him you were beautiful, formidable and not to be lied to."

"Would he lie?"

Madeline grinned. "Like a shot, if it was to his advantage. He's totally truthful only if it pays him to be."

Carol said casually, "Wilbur Shearing has a yacht, doesn't he?"

Without showing any surprise at the change of subject, Madeline detailed the vessels Wilbur Shearing owned, which ranged from an ocean-racing maxi to a prize-winning sixteen-footer he raced on Sydney Harbour.

"So he himself sails? He doesn't just employ people to do it for him?"

"It's his greatest love — next to making money, that is. Why are you asking? Are you going to tell me it's just a keen interest you have, or will it be the bit about official inquiries?"

"Just interest, I think," said Carol lightly.

Edna, the housekeeper, had set out a salad lunch in the garden. Madeline and Carol sat in green shade under an arbor hung with the branches of a broad-leaved ornamental grapevine. Carol refused wine and drank mineral water, watching Madeline with keen interest. She really was a beautiful woman, both physically and in personality. Warmly ironical, laughingly irreverent, she entertained Carol with behind-the-scenes stories from her career in television.

As they finished their meal with coffee, she leaned forward confidentially. "Carol, I want to ask you to consider an offer. Please don't just say no straight away. It's to do with a series of programs going into production now. This is quite apart from *The Shipley*

Report and I'd like you to be a consultant . . . Or, if I can persuade you, I'd like you on the screen."

"I don't think —"

"At least let me tell you a bit about it. The subject of each program is a real-life murder — not your ordinary run-of-the-mill killing, but the odd one, the bizarre case. In Australia we'll probably call it *The Aussie Way of Death* but for overseas sales the title for the series will be *Death Down Under.*"

"That's the name of a film being made now in Sydney."

Madeline nodded. "Yes, I know. Wilbur's company is involved in the movie version of *Death Down Under* and we're taking some footage for our program. Although it's been fictionalized, you know it's based on a real case, don't you?"

Carol remembered Sybil offering a copy of the script for her to read, but Carol hadn't had time to even glance at it. She said, "What real case?"

"Long before your career began. Quite sensational in the fifties. An American by the name of Ed Dowd was stationed here during the war and fell in love with a local girl. They married and he decided to stay rather than go back to the States. They had a son and adopted a daughter. About the mid-fifties they went on a motoring holiday, driving to Ayers Rock and around that area. Then they mysteriously disappeared. Car was found, but no family. Then, five years later, the body of the wife was discovered. Ed Dowd, plus his son and daughter, were never seen again."

"I think I remember reading about it. Wasn't there some suggestion of espionage?"

"Sure was," said Madeline. "It was the height of

the Cold War and Australia had Reds under every bed. Oh, and flying saucers were blamed too, not to mention obscure Aboriginal curses — you name it, every theory was explored. The fascinating thing is, of course, it's still a mystery."

The housekeeper interrupted them. "Inspector Ashton — there's a call for you."

"Take it in my study," said Madeline.

Her study was sumptuously furnished with dark furniture, and, appropriately, several television sets, video recorders and tape machines. Not one of Paul Crusoe's paintings was in evidence. The phone sat on the burgundy leather top of a huge antique desk. Carol couldn't resist sinking into the matching burgundy leather chair before she took the call.

"Thought you'd like to know," said Bourke's cheerful voice at the other end of the line, "that Syb rang you and asked for me when you weren't available. Seems while chatting to one of her students on the set she discovered something rather fascinating about Maria Kelly, and when I checked it, the information was correct . . ."

Carol was thoughtful as she replaced the receiver. It was only after Sally-Jean's death that Wilbur Shearing had been considered as a possible suspect, yet his television company had been associated with the first victim too.

She went back to Madeline, who was sipping coffee and looking reflectively over the smooth green expanse of lawn to the bordering flower beds which blended blues and mauves in a captivating muted display. Without preamble, Carol said, "Madeline, I'd like you to be cautious, because there's a possibility, a remote one, that this serial killer may have worked with you at some time. And his interest in you is disquieting anyway."

"Someone at the channel? Or can you be obliquely hinting that my boss Wilbur is a mass murderer?"

Nettled at her flippant tone, Carol said sharply, "This isn't a game. He strangles women. I don't believe you'd enjoy the experience."

Contrite, Madeline shook her head. "I'm so sorry. I get so used to dealing with tragedy, as I suppose you do, that I've learned to draw the sting with humor. Please don't think I don't take this seriously."

Although not fully convinced that Madeline gave enough weight to the warning, Carol didn't pursue the subject. She took out the photographs Bourke had had developed from the roll of film in Alissa Harvey's camera. "Would you mind glancing through these?"

Madeline shuffled through them rapidly, stopping at the photograph of herself. She viewed it through narrowed eyes. "This was taken on the set . . . probably in the last few weeks."

"How can you tell?"

"A couple of things — what I'm wearing, my hairstyle. Where did you get it?"

"It's not important, just part of our inquiries. You don't remember it being taken?"

Handing the photos back, Madeline said, "At the risk of sounding smugly self-important, I get photographed all the time. I don't remember at all."

"You don't recognize any others?"

"One's the courtyard outside my office. Otherwise, no."

Carol looked at her watch. "Madeline, I must go. Thank you for your hospitality."

"How delightfully formal you are, Carol!"

Seeing Carol to the door, Madeline added in a more serious tone, "That's a firm offer about the program. Please consider it. And you'd find it very rewarding financially, I can promise you that."

"It's not likely I'll accept."

Madeline laughed. "Sister," she said, "you ain't felt my powers of persuasion yet!"

Chapter 7

In person, Wilbur Shearing exuded the dynamic energy that characterized his frequent appearances in the public eye. He was involved in sponsorship of sporting teams, in charity organizations, and most of all in the machinations of high-flying business enterprises.

He strode across his office to shake Carol's hand. "Inspector Ashton! Great pleasure to meet you. Now, how can I help you?"

Before she could respond he had rapidly ushered her to a plumply upholstered chair, gestured to a minion to provide coffee and then sank into a matching seat to fix her with an expression that, Carol thought, nicely mingled interest and concern. He was slightly below average height, bull-necked, heavily tanned and dressed in a dark blue suit, crisp white shirt and clear red tie. His tightly curling hair was cut short to provide a dense even layer across his bulging skull.

"Now, how can I help you?" he repeated.

From newscasts she was familiar with Wilbur Shearing's idiosyncratic way of speaking, so like that used by many of his reporters on television. He spoke quite slowly, but in a series of staccato phrases, each of which contained at least one word that was emphasized, although this emphasis seemed to be almost at random. This had the effect of making everything he said sound somehow significant, however banal the meaning might be. He also had, as Bourke pointed out, a quasi-English accent. To smooth out his delivery and assume a broad Australian accent would be a very effective vocal disguise.

As Carol introduced the subject of the serial murderer Shearing's expression of concern deepened. "Shocking," he said, shaking his head. "Truly shocking. And poor Sally-Jean. What she must have gone through doesn't bear thinking about."

He leaned forward, consternation replacing mere concern. "But surely, Inspector, there's nothing more I can add on that matter, other than to say it was a dreadful tragedy and a great personal loss."

What a ham, thought Carol. She said, "We have just discovered another link to your television channel —"

He interrupted with earnest protest. "Someone in my employ? You have a suspect?"

"Not yet," said Carol, fighting to keep a frosty note from her voice. She had only been in Wilbur Shearing's company for a few minutes, yet already she felt a scornful irritation rising. He was too concerned, too eager to appear to be cooperative, too superficially responsive. "Could you tell me where you were on Tuesday evening?" she asked mildly.

"This is routine, right? And one of your officers has already checked where I was."

"Do you mind repeating it?"

"Not at all. I spent the entire evening with Edgar Boarder, my company accountant. It was at my house. We had dinner and then a rather long meeting. Business, of course."

Carol knew that Bourke had already confirmed this alibi, but she raised her eyebrows inquiringly.

He obligingly added detail. "Live at Point Piper, you know. Wanted to discuss a few matters away from the office. Edgar Boarder will be pleased to speak with you personally. He'll confirm what I've said, that we were together until almost midnight."

Edgar Boarder had so confirmed, but Mark Bourke had also pointed out that when someone who held commercial life and death over your career asked a favor, you were likely to comply. And, Bourke had added, there was the interesting coincidence that Edgar Boarder had also provided the alibi for the night of Sally-Jean's death.

As she looked at Shearing blandly, he responded with a question, "Inspector, you mentioned another link. What would that be?"

"The very first of these serial killings occurred

last December. The victim was a young woman named Maria Kelly. Quite apart from any mention in the news at the time, does her name seem familiar to you?"

She was interested in his reaction. He was leaning forward, bull neck bulging over his collar, flushed under his tan, saying emphatically, "No. Never heard it before. Should I have?"

"She was an actor. Did some work on your channel. Actually, she appeared on screen two days before she died."

"I didn't know that, of course. I would have mentioned it immediately. How is this significant, Inspector?"

"It may not be significant at all, but I would like a videotape of the program, if possible. It was, I gather, a show called *Crime Time.*"

"Ah, yes. Believe we were trying it out in the non-rating period. Didn't go ahead with it."

Carol sat forward. "You impress me, Mr. Shearing. I wouldn't have thought, with your other business interests, you'd have that kind of finely detailed information about programming, especially since it was a year ago."

His face went blank, then became animated again. "Inspector, anyone who knows me well would agree I take a hands-on approach. I do keep a close eye on program trials. Want to spot a winner if there's a winner there."

"In the same way, do Narelle Dent or Alissa Harvey strike a bell?"

He leaned back, more comfortable. "No. I know each was a victim of this dreadful strangler, but apart from that I've had nothing to do with them. Sorry I can't be of more help." He became regretful. "And that tape you wanted of *Crime Time* — we wouldn't have kept it. The concept didn't work, so there was no reason to store the pilot episodes. More than happy to check for you, but I'm sorry to say it's not likely we'll be able to help in that regard."

"Would it be possible to obtain a list of, and perhaps later speak to, the personnel who were involved in the program?"

There was a pause, then he said, a little too heartily, "But of course, Inspector! Delighted to be able to help in any way . . ."

Oh, yes? thought Carol, hiding her skepticism with a polite smile.

Sybil stood with Kirra and Malcolm watching Ripley Patterson rehearse a scene with his female co-star, Mirabelle Stone, an Australian pop singer who had some talent, dazzling dental work and an efficient publicity machine. She was now, she assured her public, branching out to include serious acting in her repertoire. Serious she might be, but Sybil had reservations about her dramatic skills, as did the director, who, scowling ferociously, was forcing her to repeat her lines over and over.

Ripley Patterson, the ultimate professional, delivered his lines exactly as required. Mirabelle Stone, however, stumbled yet again. Ripley showed no sign of annoyance or even resigned patience, going through the scene each time as though it were a fresh experience. His face was so familiar from television (he had played a cop in a long-running series) and from the big screen (he specialized in buddy movies and light romantic comedies) that Sybil found it unsettling to see it life-size, especially since in physique he was so much smaller and slighter than she had imagined . . . though, naturally, in perfect proportion.

Ripley Patterson might not have height, but he did have presence. His star quality glowed in everything about him — his regular profile, beguiling smile, thick dark hair (guiltless of even a suggestion of receding from his unlined forehead), his deeply masculine and compelling voice. Though not in the first rank of movie stars, he was assuredly in the forefront of the second line. Academy Awards nominations might evade him but his popularity with the general public was secure. He also got on well with the crew, having an uncomplicated, friendly manner. "Not up himself, like most of them," Alice had observed to Sybil, adding, "You can tell a real star, dear — they talk to everyone and don't treat themselves like something special."

However attractive he was physically, Sybil was disappointed to find him shallow and unconvincing in person, as though he had established a persona and could efficiently go through all the motions of playing him, without revealing the true personality underneath.

There was a break in the scene and Ripley came over to where Sybil, Kirra and Malcolm stood. He patted Kirra's shoulder. "Honey, would it be too much trouble to get me a coffee?" As Kirra hurried off, bright with purpose, he asked Malcolm to collect his script from his trailer. Malcolm, unimpressed by such a task, frowned heavily, but departed with a modicum of grace, since he considered Ripley Patterson to be of possible use to him when he hit the States.

Left alone, Ripley said, "Sybil, of course you'll be on the cruise tomorrow, since we all have to go, but if you're not too tired afterwards . . ." He paused to smile persuasively.

"I probably will be," she responded with a smile, to take any sting of rejection from her words.

She resented having to spend most of Saturday on Wilbur Shearing's boat, and she had protested — unavailingly — that publicity for the movie was nothing to do with her. She was now determined to at least be available to spend Saturday evening with Carol, even though it was possible Carol would be caught up in the Orange Strangler investigation.

Ripley was obviously surprised at her lack of enthusiasm for his invitation. "I've asked a few people to come back to my hotel suite for cocktails. I'd be very pleased if you'd join us."

"Syb's a very busy girl," said Charlie Date, who had come up behind them. He added in a ponderously jocular tone, "You'd be lucky to get her."

There was nothing in his voice or demeanor to cause offense, but Sybil felt a shiver of dislike. She wondered if she was being unfair — if Luke's enigmatic warning about Charlie had influenced her. She felt relieved when Vic Carbond called him over.

"Funny guy, that," said Ripley, watching Charlie as he walked away. "Hard to get to know."

Sybil smiled to herself. Perhaps the problem was that Charlie was immune to Ripley's facile charm.

She turned at a familiar but unexpected voice. "Excuse me, could you tell me where Malcolm Murtry is?"

Mark Bourke had not addressed her directly, but had made a general query. She wondered why he wasn't acknowledging the fact that they knew each other well, but she played along with him. "Malcolm? He went to fetch something. Date should be back in a moment."

Charlie Date was approaching with purpose in his bulky tread, his head thrust out belligerently. Bourke in his brown suit and beige tie stood out against the informally colorful dress of the crew. He said sharply to Bourke, "Have you some authority to be on the set? We're shooting a scene here —"

Sybil admired the way Bourke efficiently ushered Charlie out of earshot. She watched Bourke's unremarkable face and easy manner as he spoke to Charlie's unhelpfully blank stare. Then there was the showing of his credentials, a resigned shrug from Charlie and an introduction to Vic Carbond, who irritatedly waved them both away.

Luke leaned on the hand reflector he'd been holding for the scene. "Who is he?" he asked, his gaze fixed on Bourke. "Haven't seen him before."

Malcolm Murtry, who had returned with Ripley's leather-bound script under one arm, also evinced interest. "He an agent? Someone important?"

Ripley took the script with a smile. "Unless I'm much mistaken," he said, "that there person is a cop."

* * * * *

Bourke returned to Carol with Malcolm Murtry's videotape and an amused account of his experiences on *Death Down Under*'s location shooting.

"Syb took her cue and looked as though she'd never seen me before, Ripley Patterson flashed his pearlies and even I melted a bit — that guy's just too good-looking but only a shorty — and the director, our grubby little Aussie talent, Victor Carbond, grudgingly let me whip Malcolm Murtry away to collect this tape of his acting achievements."

"The crew — anyone there of interest?"

"You mean did I recognize a sex murderer or two? No, but I have the impression someone's face was familiar. Don't ask me who, because I can't quite pin it down, but it'll come to me."

Carol tried to prompt him as he put the tape into a video machine. "Come on Mark. Man or woman? Recent or a long time ago? Crim? Victim?"

"Don't bully me, Carol. I'll remember, just give me time." He pressed the play button. "We owe a lot to Malcolm Murtry, child star," he said, "since it's his ego that's preserved this scene. As Shearing told you, the channel telecast this and another pilot in the series, decided to junk the idea and destroyed the masters. This is probably the only copy around."

The screen crackled with gray lines, then leaped into brightly colored life. *"Crime Time,"* intoned a male voice-over full of portent. This was followed by a rather uncomfortable introduction to the program by a then-popular quiz show host, who had since disappeared from the entertainment scene.

"Wonder what happened to him?" said Bourke idly. "No talent, but great teeth. Got him a long way in the short term."

"Probably bit off more than he could chew."

Bourke shot her a grin. "Unkind," he said, "since the attrition rate in television is pure murder. Only a few ever to get to the top and stay there, like your friend Madeline Shipley. And, Carol, they have to be ruthless to do it. You know the whole thing she's feeding us about the calls could be a con. After all, it is an important rating period at the moment."

"There's Malcolm," said Carol as his sulky good looks appeared on the screen. The item was a re-enactment of a crime and both recognized it immediately.

"The Fernandez shooting," said Bourke.

Kerry Fernandez had been an abused wife, married to an outwardly smooth but inwardly raging businessman of some influence. The young couple had exuded success, living in an exclusive part of Sydney, both of them serving on boards of charities, appearing regularly in the social pages with the right people. Then one evening Kerry Fernandez had blown her husband's head off with her birthday gift to him, an expensive engraved shotgun intended for clay pigeon shooting.

All this was sensation enough, but there was an added ironic twist that excited the media further. Fernandez had recently been appointed to chair a government inquiry set up to assess domestic violence and to present a report and recommendations to parliament. For the head of such an inquiry to be a wife-beater himself, and for the said wife to dispatch him with a shotgun that was her birthday gift to him, was a media delight.

The pilot program Carol and Bourke were watching had obviously been devoted to the subject of the Fernandez murder because of these sensational aspects. In the re-enactment of the crime, Maria Kelly was cast as Kerry Fernandez, and her husband was played by a familiar but mediocre actor whose continued career was testament to the power of good connections in the entertainment industry. Malcolm Murtry had his big moment in the small role of the young neighbor who heard the shot, rushed in to help, and was confronted by a calm Mrs. Fernandez who handed him the shotgun and went to ring the police herself.

Carol watched Maria Kelly with a feeling of angry sadness. She acted well, but it was more than that. She projected a glowing vulnerability that was strangely compelling.

Bourke felt it too. "Jesus," he said, "why choose her to kill? What harm could she have ever done anyone?"

"Maybe she represents the unattainable. Just being female might be enough, but I think there's more than that. Whatever it is, we've got to find it."

Bourke looked grim. "I'm seeing Alissa Harvey's parents again this evening," he said. "Maybe they'll give us something."

Carol let the tape run through. The program was followed by a second, also featuring Malcolm Murtry, but this time in an even smaller part, where he was merely required to fall wounded to the floor.

Bourke grimaced as it ended. "I hate those," he said, "where they kill their children. Suicide, that's fine . . . but why murder your family?"

They watched the tape through twice more in silence.

Carol said, "I want to know if any of the other

96

victims have any association at all with Kerry Fernandez. And the names of everyone who in any way had anything to do with *Crime Time*."

"You know Kerry Fernandez has appealed against her life sentence. It's due to be heard soon."

"Yes, Mark, that's got to be checked out — anyone associated with the committee who lobbied for her sentence to be set aside. And any of her husband's relatives who might have a grudge. See if there could be any possible link with the inquiry Fernandez was chairing on domestic violence."

Mark was scribbling notes. "I'll put a team on each area straight away. Can I beef up the group feeding details into the computer? This is going to be a nightmare to cross-reference."

"You'll get as many people as you need. Just ask. And Mark, this time don't miss a thing."

He didn't protest her criticism. After Malcolm Murtry had mentioned Maria Kelly's appearance in the crime re-enactment Bourke had gone back over the files and found a passing reference to her last acting role. It was just one point in the crowding details that made up the investigation of a victim's life and it had been given no importance. Both Carol and Bourke knew how often a vital piece of information was hidden in a welter of information, only to be picked up by chance.

He said mildly, "This still could mean nothing, Carol."

"We're not exactly overwhelmed with leads," she observed, "and I do like to keep you busy, Mark."

As he was leaving her office, she said, *"Death Down Under* — I want a check on the names of the crew. All of them. You'll find some cross-check with the channel because they're on loan from Shearing Media."

He grinned at her. "And La Shipley's staff as well?"

"Why not. And double-check her husband, Paul Crusoe."

"Good choice," said Bourke. "There *is* a certain artistry in the presentation of the bodies."

Friday evening. Thunder growled in the dark sky. Lightning licked along the horizon, flickering against the massing clouds.

Sybil, relaxed in jeans and an ancient T-shirt, frowned over her cooking. Carol poured generous whiskeys. Jeffrey and Sinker complained of neglect.

"This is ridiculous," said Carol to the cats. "It's obvious your internal clocks are out of kilter. Dinner isn't due for an hour yet."

They remained unconvinced. As she collected their dishes she said to Sybil, "Tell me about the gossip on the set . . . For example, has anyone shown a deep interest in discussing the Orange Strangler?"

Sybil looked up from her cookbook. *Italian Gourmet Cooking Made Easy* its title claimed, although she was fast gaining doubts. "The topic's come up. After all, it's on the news every night. Why?"

Carol was offhand. "Faint chance there might be a lead because the film company's an offshoot of Shearing Media. We've found two of the victims had some link in some way with the channel."

98

"Well, Alice Fleming's had a field day with the subject, but that's nothing unusual because she loves anything spicy or scandalous."

"What sort of thing does she say?"

"Nothing original. Mostly repeats what she's read or seen on television. She particularly likes to speculate on what would make someone get a charge out of killing women."

Interested, Carol said, "What's her theory?"

Sybil grinned. "Can best be summed up as the Small-Dick-Tiny-Balls theory of motivation. He feels inferior and can't get a girl, so he has his revenge on all women."

"Do any of the men you work with fit that general description?"

Sybil chuckled. "A poorly equipped, but crazed misogynist?"

Carol smiled, but with an edge of anger. She thought of Madeline's similar flippant response. "It's a particularly nasty way to die, to be throttled. And his next victim is walking round right now, maybe joking about the Orange Strangler."

Immediately serious, Sybil instinctively put her hand to her throat. "Yes, it's horrible. But you never think it'll happen to you, or to someone you know."

A wail from the cats reminded Carol of her duties. Sinker led the way to the deck followed by Carol bearing two dinners and Jeffrey bringing up the rear.

The wind was rising, buffeting the trees and scattering twigs and gumnuts along the deck. There was a wild, electric feeling in the air. Thunder grumbled irritably along the western skyline and the cats, usually exemplary in their concentration on their food bowls, twitched and flicked their tails.

"Going to be a humdinger of a storm," she observed as she came inside.

It was the kind of night beloved of thriller writers, where unmentionable things happened as lightning and thunder provided a theatrical background. Carol again felt a prickle of fear for Sybil's safety. She said casually, "Darling, you won't ever think of taking a lift with anyone from the crew, will you? Man or woman."

"It is a he?"

"Probably. Both Mark and I keep saying he or she but I think we both believe it's a he."

Carol asked her about her impressions of the film crew. Sybil gave brief character sketches and her overall impressions, adding, "And not one of them strikes me as being straightjacket material — I don't mean everyone is sweetness and light, but no one seems to be even slightly psycho."

"He won't. Almost certainly he appears to be an ordinary person."

"Speaking of rather more than ordinary persons," said Sybil with a teasing grin, "Ripley Patterson's asked me to his hotel suite tomorrow night after the harbor cruise."

"Well," said Carol, mockingly impressed, "that's an opportunity you wouldn't want to miss."

Smiling at her tone, Sybil said, "It's a party, it's not just little me. I was vague about whether I'd go, and I'll definitely give it a miss if you're going to be home . . ."

"It's a date. What time do you escape from Shearing's pleasure cruiser?"

"About five, I think. Carol, you know I don't want to waste a whole day on the harbor when we

100

could be together, but quite apart from the fact I tried to get out of it and couldn't, I don't suppose you'd have the luxury of a Saturday at home anyhow."

Carol sighed. "I'm taking Sunday off because it's David's birthday. Mark Bourke is working right through the weekend and so are a lot of other people. I'll be here tomorrow when you get home, but you know what it's like in the middle of an investigation . . ."

Sybil was unsuccessful in suppressing the complaint in her voice. "I know how many times you say you'll be here, and then you ring and say sorry, something's come up."

Carol stood behind her, put her arms about her waist, hugged her gently. She said softly against her neck, "These days if I don't turn up on schedule, I never see you. You're always out shooting or tutoring, or junketing around the harbor on a publicity cruise."

Sybil turned in her arms. "Am I so unreasonable?" she asked. "I miss being with you. We need to spend time together."

Carol let her arms drop, resenting the demands Sybil was making. Why did she need to justify the time she spent on the job? She said emphatically, "There's someone out there who likes killing. It brings him attention. It puffs up his ego. It makes him feel important and powerful. And soon he'll need another fix, another victim. I promised to be home with you tonight, but if there was any new lead, I wouldn't be."

Sybil obviously wanted to step back from the argument that could be precipitated so easily. She

101

said conversationally, "You must have some suspects. Have you narrowed it down to a short list?"

Carol laughed without amusement. "Sure," she said, "whittled it down to about half the population of Sydney. And that's not taking into account the fact he might fly in from another state, kill a selected victim, then fly out again. Basically, it's a fairly long short list, you might say."

Chapter 8

Carol was sitting up in bed talking on the phone when Sybil awoke. Admiring the smooth, lightly tanned curve of her back, the swing of her blonde hair, the strong line of her jaw, Sybil rolled over to run her fingers down Carol's stomach.

Carol grabbed her hand, holding it tightly as she continued the conversation. When she replaced the receiver she said severely, "Sybil, I do wish you'd keep your hands to yourself. Surely you can't think a cry of ecstasy in the middle of an official call would be well received?"

"Who was it? Don't tell me the prime minister?"

"Mark."

"He'd understand."

Carol smiled, but she wondered if he would. Although he well knew Sybil and Carol's relationship, she always felt he was slightly embarrassed about it. He joked about many things, but never ever about gay women, at least not in her hearing. When he had told her about Mr. and Mrs. Harvey's shamefaced revelation to him yesterday evening that their dead daughter had been a lesbian, he had sounded awkward and uncomfortable.

She consulted a number, dialed. "Madeline? It's Carol Ashton. Did I wake you? I have a favor to ask . . ."

Sybil sat on the edge of the bed, watching her frown. She had learned to read Carol's expressions well. This morning she was abstracted, concentrated, turning aside from anything or anyone that might divert her attention.

Abandoning plans for affectionate wrestling, Sybil left her talking and went into the kitchen to prime Carol's battered coffee percolator. Then she distributed breakfast to the beady-eyed contingent of birds, mainly magpies and kookaburras who had assembled in family groups for sustenance.

The tempest of rain last night had washed the air clean, but littered the deck with fragments of gumleaf, bark and little branches. Far below, the normally blue-green waters of Middle Harbour were khaki-colored with dirt washed from the steeply rising slopes. She stretched luxuriously, delighting in the early sun and the thought of a relaxed day on the harbor.

Carol followed her out, a black kimono accentuating the paleness of her hair. "I'm going to be on the catamaran ferry with you today . . . well, not actually with you, but as Madeline Shipley's guest . . . and I'd rather you didn't —"

Sybil didn't bother to disguise her irritation. "All right. We'll be total strangers." Carol's patient expression only increased her annoyance. "Look," Sybil snapped, "we could be friends, you know. We don't have to be lovers just because we know each other."

"Sybil, there's every chance that the serial murderer will be one of the people sharing the boat with us. He knows I'm investigating the murders. I don't want anything to tie you to me. It would be too dangerous."

Mollified by the explanation, Sybil said, "You've got a strong lead? A name?"

Carol shook her head ruefully. "Not one name, but names. Cross-referenced to two or more of the victims. Could be a blind alley, but I want to meet them on neutral ground, where there's no apparent threat."

"Carol, everyone knows you. If he is on the boat, he'll be on his guard. He'll know you're there looking for him."

"Not at all. Madeline will be announcing that I'm becoming involved as a consultant for a new series on crime she's producing for Wilbur Shearing's media company. I'll just be there for publicity reasons."

Sybil had time to feel surprised hurt that Carol hadn't shared this with her before as she said, "Is it true?"

"That she's offered me a role in her new series?

Yes, but I doubt if I'll actually take it up. It's a convenient, and checkable, cover. That's why I'm using it."

The catamaran, dazzling in the sunlight with clean white paint and the metal shine of aluminum, edged delicately up to Kirribilli wharf, *Spirit of the Wind V* blazoned in italic script along each side.

The day was perfect, the sun obligingly highlighting the beauty of Sydney Harbour while not creating more than a pleasant warmth. Yachts, ferries and heavily-laden container ships slid on their appointed paths, seagulls squawked and wheeled and overhead a few fat white clouds added interest to the pale blue wash of the sky.

"We should go separately," Carol had said to Sybil, leaving Seaforth early to drive to Madeline's place at Hunters Hill. She was to pick her up and then drive into the city to join the cruiser on the southern side of the harbor at Man of War Jetty beside the spectacular bulk of the Sydney Opera House.

On the opposite shore, Sybil became part of the contingent who parked their cars near the huge stone northern pylons of the Harbour Bridge and trooped down the curling concrete path to Kirribilli Wharf.

As she was locking her car Luke West put an arm around her waist. "Syb! Come and splice the mainbrace with me, eh?"

Charlie Date had parked behind her and he waited, smoothing his moustache with a careful forefinger, for them to join him. Instead of his usual loose shirt and comfortably shabby pants he was wearing an all-denim outfit that looked slightly incongruous on his bulging body. In contrast, Luke was trim in tailored shorts and long socks.

They accompanied her down to the wharf, their contrasting styles making her feel like the meat in an unequal sandwich.

She went on automatic pilot, making appropriate responses to Luke's conversational gambits as she looked with appreciation at her city. Working on a film set had made her view each scene with measuring eyes, so she framed it in an imaginary lens. Across the coruscating blue of the water, the buildings of Sydney made a mini New York and, leaping from the gigantic sandstone pylons near the path, the Harbour Bridge stretched gray metal ribs against the pale sky. The waiting catamaran was space-age in its chunky, functional lines.

Intended for serious business entertainment, the cruiser was outfitted as an elaborate floating restaurant and conference venue. *Spirit of the Wind* was Shearing's name for all his vessels, of whatever size or function. Sybil remembered his maxi-yacht *Spirit of the Wind III* winning the Sydney to Hobart ocean race a few years before.

Wilbur Shearing was standing in expansive joviality by the gangplank, alert to the impression he gave to the carefully selected media representatives and public relations consultants he had assembled. Sybil recognized Madeline Shipley beside him, and she, in turn, after a close look, smiled and said, "Sybil Quade. How nice to meet you. Carol, of course, has said nothing at all about you."

She was conscious that Luke and Charlie stood behind her, listening. Utterly disconcerted, Sybil said abruptly, "Why would she?"

Madeline gave a little shake of her head to indicate polite puzzlement at Carol's omission. "Sybil, I'd be so pleased if you and Carol would come to dinner, soon. My husband Paul is not here today — he can't bear this sort of occasion — but I know he will be as delighted to meet you as I am."

Sybil had regained her equilibrium. She said pleasantly, "I was a little taken aback you recognized me. I can't imagine why you should."

"I'm afraid I have a long memory for people who appear in the news . . ."

Sybil thought, Is she too courteous to add I was a suspect in a double murder, or is she just playing with me?

A clump of people were coming up the gangplank, so Sybil murmured a polite phrase and allowed herself to be swept along with them. She looked back to see Madeline staring after her, an enigmatic smile on her lips.

Luke was caught up in a conversation, but Charlie stuck to Sybil's side. "Who's this Carol?" he asked.

She made her voice casual. "A mutual friend, that's all," she said vaguely. She made an excuse and pushed her way through a knot of people, leaving him behind. She looked for Carol, but couldn't see her. What should she do? Warn Carol? Do nothing?

Alice grabbed her arm. "Syb, dear, come and have some champagne with us! It's free *and* French — could you ask for anything more?"

Deciding that she would only speak to Carol if an

easy opportunity presented itself, Sybil pushed the anxiety she felt to the back of her mind and allowed herself to be led away.

Wilbur Shearing was making a speech. Minions shushed guests insensitive enough to still be engrossed in personal conversation, the staff behind the large circular bar took the opportunity to relax against the chromium-edged counter, tame photographers ducked and clicked sychophantically.

"Ladies and gentlemen . . . or should I say, since Shearing Media Corporation is, of course, an equal opportunity employer . . . men and women . . ."

He paused for the polite titter of laughter that his audience knew he expected, then launched into the meat of his speech. He warmly thanked certain members of the print and electronic media for their presence, ignoring those from his own companies, as they didn't need to be stroked with warm words to encourage favorable coverage. He made extravagant reference to the independence of the Australian Broadcasting Corporation, which had sent along a team to film the cruise under the guise of gathering material for yet another of their programs devoted to how Australians were selling Australia to the world and wasn't that a Good Thing.

Shearing's gestures became more expansive, his delivery more emphatic, as he began to enumerate his personal achievements in, it seemed, single-handedly revitalizing the Australian film industry. He introduced Vic Carbond as a director of vision and creativity. Carbond, dressed in a light-colored, crumpled and rather grubby suit, mumbled a few incoherent words and then returned to his beer.

Then it was time to parade the stars. First Mirabelle Stone, attired gorgeously in very little, who offered a few ingenuous comments, followed by Malcolm Murtry wearing impossibly tight leather pants and a red shirt open to show a generous area of tanned chest. He was quite prepared to speak for some time on his personal contribution to the performing arts in Australia, but was nudged aside by Shearing, who showed great delight in introducing his trump card, international movie star Ripley Patterson.

Dressed in flawlessly white jeans and a nautical top, Ripley gave the polished performance he must have delivered many times before. He smiled and made modest comments in his attractively resonant voice, emphasizing how much he loved Australia, loved working in Australia, regarded Australia as his second home. He spoke glowingly of the technical abilities of the local film industry, his warm glance encompassing the members of his film crew as he spoke.

"Isn't he great!" hissed Alice Fleming in Sybil's reluctant ear. "I just love him! What a guy!"

There was a ripple of interest as Madeline Shipley rose to speak. She stood relaxed yet self-contained, in an admirably cut jumpsuit of moss green and gold that on anyone else might have looked a little too extreme, but on her struck the right note of casual elegance.

Helen Tolsten stood to one side, ready to hand her speech notes, a glass of water — anything Madeline might need. Madeline needed nothing. She caught her audience in a moment and held them as she spoke clearly, wittily and concisely about the entertainment industry in general, and Shearing Media Corporation in particular. She concluded by mentioning that both she and Wilbur Shearing had warm hopes that Detective Inspector Carol Ashton, who was present on the cruise today (heads turned to locate Carol, who ignored the stares and kept her gaze politely on the speaker), would shortly be involved as a consultant in an exciting new program to be produced by Shearing Media. She could not give details as yet, but hoped an announcement could be made in the next few weeks.

Wilbur Shearing returned to announce that a buffet lunch would be available immediately. The bar staff revved themselves up to meet the onslaught of drinkers denied alcohol for the duration of the speeches, and Carol smiled at Ripley Patterson, careful not to tower over him.

"You've visited Australia before?" she said conversationally.

He had, and was pleased to elaborate with practiced ease. While he spoke Carol assessed him. She felt he was acting the part of Ripley Patterson, Movie Star, and not with very much commitment. There was a touch of weariness in his enthusiasm, an edge of boredom in his hearty comments about the great opportunities Australia offered him.

Carol thought, I wonder if that includes the opportunity to murder?

Bourke had investigated Ripley Patterson's various trips to Australia. Not only had he been in the country when each of the murders had occurred, he had always been in Sydney at the time. Bourke had added on the phone that morning, "Plenty of publicity stuff about his affairs with various models etcetera, but the word is that he's a queer."

At Carol's exasperated sigh, he had cleared his throat and said, "Did I say queer? Meant gay, Carol, of course. Anyway, if he *is* gay, maybe he's one who doesn't like women. L.A. has sent us something interesting. Film star Ripley was up for assault on a female before he made the big time. Two counts. Waiting for the full details, but it looks a bit promising, doesn't it?"

Carol chatted inconsequentially with Ripley and observed him closely. He was, as Mark had observed to her, a "shorty" but he had a beautifully proportioned body with a tight narrow waist any woman would envy. His skin was evenly tanned, his dark eyes sparkled with laughter, and all in all it was difficult to imagine him attacking anyone, let alone a woman.

Carol knew that pride was the Achilles heel of many murderers, particularly those who had completely evaded suspicion. If he was the Orange Strangler, she wanted to give him an opportunity to gloat. She said, "You live in Los Angeles, I believe? How does it compare to Sydney? Do you feel L.A. is more violent? More exciting?" Before he could answer, she added, laughing, "Be honest now, Ripley! I'm a police officer, not a PR person."

He laughed in turn. "You're right," he said, "I know all the things to say for public record . . . how I love the country, the people, the lifestyle . . . However, as far as Australia's concerned, it's absolutely true. And frankly, I feel safer here in Sydney than I do back home."

"We have crime here, too."

"Yeah, and some of it pretty bizarre. You're working on the strangler case, aren't you?"

Yes! thought Carol. Do you want to talk about the Orange Strangler? She played with the bait, adopting a rueful tone. "Yes, I've just come on to the case. He's clever, or very lucky. We're nowhere near him."

He was showing the correct reactions — interest, even fascination, but no hidden exultation that she could sense, no amused superiority.

"Sorry to interrupt," said Helen Tolsten abruptly, "but Madeline wants you to meet Vic Carbond."

And what Madeline wants, you deliver, thought Carol as she followed Helen's confident briskness.

Sybil had escaped the plenitude of conversation and artificial goodwill to take the pleasure of wind in her hair and the soothing sight of the water being sliced into a mild wake by the two huge metal floats that supported the vessel.

There was a chill in the salty breeze and so she found herself alone on the outer area of the upper deck. The catamaran was skimming serenely, effortlessly overtaking other vessels. She narrowed her eyes against the wind and enjoyed the changing patterns of sea, sky and land. It was with irritation that she realized she had been tracked down.

"Syb," said Luke West, looking serious, "when we came on board I overheard Madeline Shipley mention you were once on the news."

With an effort Sybil kept her face expressionless.

Luke continued, "I just want you to know I won't say anything, especially to Alice. The very first time I saw you I recognized you . . . The case was really given a beating on TV. I'm just surprised no one else's tumbled to who you are."

She made her voice offhand. "It's old news."

"Maybe it is, but I can just see what Alice Fleming could make of it, can't you?"

She looked at him sharply, wondering if he was enjoying the possibility of a little gentle blackmail and would shortly be suggesting what she might do for him, but he met her eyes with innocent concern.

"It's hard, isn't it? Someone, somewhere, will always remember."

She made a noncommittal sound, wanting him to drop the subject.

"I hate them," he said, "those bloodsuckers who live on other people's misery."

Carol avoided shaking hands with Vic Carbond. She had read his dossier and knew the details of his sleazy life. Talented he undoubtedly was, but he had used much of that talent in producing a stream of cheap X-rated movies, many of them featuring young illegal immigrants of both sexes. He had never been charged, had never actually fallen into the sewer, but he was tainted with the corruption that comes from exploitation of the most bestial side of human nature. Interestingly, it appeared that Carbond had asked Madeline to approach Carol for him. After a few preparatory comments, the reason became clear.

"You're on the Orange Strangler case," he said.

She nodded a cool agreement as he ran a hand through his greasy hair. "Interesting," he said, "serial murder. People love it. There's no rape, though, is there?"

Thinking he might be disappointed at this lack of ultimate violence, she said firmly, "No."

"I'm interested in a film project — when you catch him, of course. Remember the film on the Boston Strangler? Thinking of doing it along those lines. There's something in it for both of us, Inspector. What I mean is, you give me the information, you know, all the stuff that doesn't get in the papers, the good oil. And I pay you as a consultant. Your name doesn't have to appear. No one has to know, if that's the way you want it." He paused. "Know what I mean?"

She knew what he meant. She repressed the scathing comments that rose in her mouth and said mildly, "So you have a particular interest in the Orange Strangler. Why is that?"

"I told you. People love it. And they like the way he thumbs his nose at you, the cops. Bores it up you. Laughs at you."

She couldn't be sure his glee at the failure of the police wasn't just from his own life experiences of skating near to arrest. But then, if he was the Orange Strangler, this conversation would give him a charge like no other — to openly, and safely, discuss with the head of the police team hunting him the way he was making fools of them.

She didn't accept his offer. She didn't refuse it. She continued to chat with him, blandly, until Helen Tolsten came to summon her away again.

115

* * * * *

"I'm rescuing you," said Madeline, opening the door to a small private cabin aft. "This is Wilbur's retreat, of course, but he's out massaging the egos of the media for all he's worth, so we have it to ourselves."

Carol followed her into a room which was small, but luxuriously appointed. Madeline handed her a drink from the bar set into the wall and they both sank into upholstered swivel chairs.

"I'd better come clean before you speak to your Sybil," said Madeline, her tone self-satisfied.

Carol grew alert at the slight emphasis on *your*, but she kept her face still.

Madeline frowned playfully. "Come on, aren't you even going to look suitably impressed?"

"At what?"

"That I remembered who Sybil Quade is."

Carol moved impatiently, alarm growing in her mind. She said coldly, "I doubt you did remember Sybil. I'd be more likely to think you had me researched. That's about it, isn't it?"

Madeline smiled ruefully. "You're right, but Carol, you do it all the time — research people, I mean."

Bitter anger that Madeline should have her at such a disadvantage made Carol's voice harsh. "Researching people's my job."

"Well, it's mine too."

Carol thought, Did you dig up everything? That I fell in love with a woman, left my influential husband, abandoned my son? What a pretty story that would make for your bloody program. She said disdainfully, "Unless you're intending to do an exposé of my life, you did it out of curiosity."

"You're angry with me?"

Carol said, her tone flat, "I'm furious."

Madeline leaned forward, put her hand on Carol's arm and said persuasively, "Carol, I'm not going to announce on air that you're living in a lesbian relationship."

"Thanks be for such mercies."

Madeline looked genuinely surprised at her bitter tone. "I thought we were friends . . ."

Are you doing this for sport? thought Carol. She said, "Did you get Helen Tolsten to do the digging?"

"Well, yes. I don't have the time . . ."

Carol drained her drink, stood up, put the glass down with a crack on the polished table. She felt like making threats, taking Madeline Shipley by the throat, breaking something.

Instead, she walked calmly out of the room, closing the door firmly behind her.

"Inspector? Inspector Ashton?"

Carol stopped, turning the flame off underneath her anger.

"I'm Malcolm, Malcolm Murtry. Your Detective Bourke saw me yesterday. About the videotape. I knew Maria Kelly. Remember?"

"Of course. How can I help you, Mr. Murtry?"

Malcolm looked surprised. "Well," he said, "thought you'd be looking for me. Want to question me yourself, personally."

"Detective Sergeant Bourke interviewed you yesterday. Have you more to add to what you told him?"

"But you're in charge, aren't you? I mean, I saw it on TV, how you were taking over, like. Isn't it true, then?"

"I'm overseeing the entire investigation. Yes, that's true."

He was visibly disappointed. "So you don't want to see me."

"I'd be very interested in your impressions, Mr. Murtry . . ."

This was invitation enough. "Well," he said, taking her arm and drawing her to one side, "I was just starting out . . . I'd done things before, of course, but my agent, Tim Ogly . . ." There was a pause, apparently for Carol to be impressed by his association with this particular agent, then he continued, "He was Maria's too, I suppose you know — well, he said this part for me . . ."

Carol let him describe his career in tiresome detail as she mentally checked back over Maria Kelly's file. She couldn't remember any mention of an agent, but the sheer avalanche of unrelated and usually insignificant facts about a murder victim could hide nuggets of worth. She was interested enough to question him about *Crime Time.*

"I've answered all these questions before," he protested.

Finally, apparently deciding he had exhausted Carol's possibilities, he made moves to go. She said, idly, "The other victims of the Orange Strangler — did you know any of them?"

"Not know, exactly. I saw the old one on TV once, before it all happened."

"The old one? Do you mean Narelle Dent? She was thirty-three."

He grinned, a little abashed. "Yeah, well, that's pretty old to me. The one who was a check-out chick, or something."

Carol was intrigued. "You mean she was on television before she was killed, before all the publicity about her murder?"

"Yeah, that's right. I remember being surprised to see her again . . . when she was dead, if you see what I mean."

"Why was she on television? What sort of program was it?"

He shrugged. "Search me. She wasn't acting, or anything like that. Would have remembered if she'd been in a drama, or something."

Further questioning got Carol no further. Malcolm was positive it was Narelle Dent he had seen, but he couldn't remember in what context. He became rapidly bored when the topic of conversation was not himself, and eventually Carol let him go.

As he walked away she said, "One more thing . . . do you drive a car?"

"Well, I'm not old enough to have a license, if that's what you mean."

"Can you drive?"

Malcolm smiled at her cockily. "What'd you expect?" he said. "Sure I can."

Chapter 9

Carol watched Sybil's red hair as most of the passengers left the catamaran at Kirribilli wharf. She half-raised her hand to wave as Sybil looked back at the vessel, but then dropped her arm as she realized Wilbur Shearing was standing beside her.

They chatted in a desultory way as *Spirit of the Wind V* skimmed efficiently across the harbor to the city. He looked immensely pleased with himself, a satisfaction mirrored in his self-laudatory conversation. She was content to let him do most of the talking as she mentally tried him out in the role of serial murderer, but she found it hard to imagine he needed to live a double life, so obviously delighted was he with the one in public view. He shared one likely characteristic with the murderer — an extremely healthy, if not monumental, ego — but that was probably an essential requirement for any very successful entrepreneur.

As they docked at Man of War Jetty, he excused himself to go smile upon those media luminaries still to leave the vessel. She watched with ironic amusement from the upper deck as he glad-handed a group of them along the gangplank and up the steps, his rather short legs hurrying to keep up.

Madeline caught Carol's arm as she went to disembark. "Carol, I'm sorry. I wouldn't have upset you for the world. I've been stupid and thoughtless and I hope you'll forgive me."

Carol moved away from her touch, saying coldly, "Then why did you find it necessary to look into my private life?"

Madeline was smiling regretfully. "I suspect the answer will make you even madder than you are already. It's just second nature to me to ask for a background briefing. I didn't think twice . . . Well, to be honest, I *was* a little curious about you, I suppose because you have such a high profile public life, but nothing at all is ever said about who you really are."

Her voice a challenge, Carol said, "So now you know."

"Carol, of course I don't *know*. All I have is some details — not the truth about the real person behind the facts."

Carol said cynically, "And here was I thinking you were preparing material for a program on me . . .

something along the lines of 'Top Cop's Secret Life' . . . but all the time it was just a friendly interest on your part."

Helen Tolsten was approaching with hard-faced efficiency. "Madeline, there's a call for you in Mr. Shearing's private cabin — it's important and confidential."

Madeline dismissed Helen's message with a nod, saying urgently to Carol, "I have to talk to you. There's something we need to discuss. I'll call you later, okay?"

Helen Tolsten stared at her, face blank, then turned to follow Madeline.

Carol watched her with narrowed eyes, conscious of a rage that was all the deeper because it was impotent.

Mark Bourke was waiting when Carol walked into his office. He made a visible effort to throw off the fatigue that had deepened the lines bracketing his mouth. "How'd it go?"

"Interesting. And rather like you on the set of *Death Down Under,* I've got a nagging feeling I've seen someone today who I should remember for some reason. Don't suppose you've come up with the mystery face yourself?"

He gestured at the piles of paper crowding his desk. "Haven't given it another thought. Got enough to do trying to keep up with the paperwork here."

"Speaking of which, what've we got on Malcolm Murtry?"

"Malcolm Murtry, teenage sex symbol? Not much, he hasn't lived long enough."

"We've had murderers much younger than he."

Bourke was hunting through a pile of folders. "Maybe," he said, "but not serial killers like this. Still, I suppose there's got to be a first time, and he's certainly got the ego."

"He told me he thought he'd seen Narelle Dent on television some time before she died, but he couldn't remember why, where or when."

Bourke scribbled a note on a pad. "Okay, I'll check that. Now, here's all we've been able to get so far on our boy Malcolm . . ."

Malcolm Murtry had been christened Dennis Malcolm Murtry nearly sixteen years before. His mother had deserted the family when he was three, leaving Malcolm and an elder brother, Shane, to be brought up by their father. There was no record of any juvenile offenses for either of the boys. The father was a hard-working tradesman and both sons still lived with him, although Shane was shortly to marry and leave home. Malcolm had insisted on changing to his second name when he had his first taste of show business after an aunt working in an advertising agency had arranged for him to appear in a television commercial for toothpaste.

"Hasn't actually had a meteoric rise to fame," said Bourke, "but he's a good-looking kid and he got himself an agent and pushed himself at every opportunity. This movie's the biggest break he's had."

"I want you to check the agent. His name's Tim Ogly and Malcolm said he represented Maria Kelly too."

"Yes, Ogly did represent her. I've already talked to him. He runs his own talent agency, specializes in the young and inexperienced. There's nothing shady, he's just a bit of a con man."

Carol leaned back thoughtfully. "Who did Malcolm Murtry's portfolio of publicity photos? Someone through Ogly, or a free lance?"

"That's a thought, Carol. You're hoping it was Alissa Harvey, eh?"

"A long shot, but give it a go."

She asked for the full details on Bourke's second meeting with Alissa Harvey's parents. Interviewing the distressed relatives of murder victims was one of the most stressful parts of an investigation, and she knew Bourke had had to struggle to distance himself from their grief and bewilderment. His voice had little intonation as he recited his questions and their answers.

Alissa was the Harvey's only daughter. There was also a younger son. She had been brought up in a firmly Christian household with very strict and conventional views on life and morality. They had been pleased that she was making a career for herself as a gifted photographer, but regarded this activity as just a prelude to marriage and children.

At nineteen Alissa told them of her lesbianism. Her father and mother were shocked and confused. Where had they gone wrong, that their daughter would turn to such God-denying behavior? They argued, prayed, sought professional help. Alissa stubbornly refused to recant. The whole issue had become a source of conflict and sorrow, but they loved their daughter and when she moved out of their home they continued to see her regularly.

Mrs. Harvey had sobbed as she said to Bourke, "Alissa died in sin, still believing that what she was doing was right. In time she would have realized, but that man who killed her took away any chance that she would grow to understand how she was sinning against God."

They had both begged him, if it was possible, to keep the fact that Alissa had been gay out of the media. "It's her brother, John. He didn't really understand about Alissa's lifestyle. He's shattered by her death and to learn about her now — that would be too much for him to bear."

Bourke said soberly to Carol, "I've told them we'll do our best but I can't promise anything. I explained there's too many people who could talk — friends, lovers, someone who gets a charge out of being in the know . . ."

Uneasily aware that there was a measure of hypocrisy in her words, Carol said, "It would be better if they told their son straight out, rather than let him find out about his sister some other way. Then, what would it matter — if they loved their daughter . . ." She was appalled to find her eyes stinging with tears. How facile, how slick she sounded — and she was speaking about a young woman who had had the courage to face her parents with the truth.

Bourke seemed not to notice her discomfiture. He looked dispirited and tired. He brightened when Carol changed the subject by asking for the details on

Ripley Patterson. Bourke handed her a schedule of the movie star's visits to Australia. "Patterson's been in Sydney for most of the past year, first to shoot a couple of episodes of a spy series, then for some commercials and lastly for *Death Down Under.*"

"Got the full details on his assault charges?"

Bourke handed her a fax printout. "It's all there. Nothing startling. Basically he roughed up a girlfriend a couple of times."

"I thought you said he was gay."

Bourke shrugged. "Maybe he swings both ways. Maybe she was meant to be a cover. Or maybe he took a while to find out where his true interests lay."

He slid his eyes away from her, and she was suddenly aware he was thinking of her marriage and later, her women lovers.

She spoke decisively. "Mark, this is ridiculous. Every time you mention anything to do with homosexuality you look uncomfortable. Do you think I'm waiting to take things the wrong way — listening to see if I can discover you making a dig at me? Or is it that I embarrass you?"

He was stung by her last comment, saying emphatically, "Embarrass me? No, never!"

"What is it then?"

He paused, then grinned slightly. "I suppose I'm taking my cue from you. I always get the impression you tense up every time the subject's mentioned. Maybe I'm wrong . . ."

Carol looked at him directly, aware that, for her, evasion was becoming less of an option. "You're not wrong, Mark. I just have trouble facing the truth, but I'm working on it."

There was a long silence between them, but not an awkward one.

Bourke said, "I've got some information on Paul Crusoe's silent number. Do you want it now?"

At her nod Bourke went through the list of those who had been given the number — Crusoe's family and friends, some business acquaintances, and, of course, his wife.

"Madeline Shipley apparently isn't willing to give this unlisted number to anyone in the entertainment business," he explained, "because, as the steely Ms. Tolsten, her assistant, stated — she values her privacy. Thought it a bit of a laugh, Carol, since La Shipley's entire career is built on delving into other people's lives, but still . . ."

"So no one at Shearing Media has the number?"

"Wilbur Shearing does. Madeline's assistant does. And since in each case Ferguson reported the number's written down for all to find, I don't imagine it would be very difficult to discover it if you wanted to."

"There's a tap on the line, of course."

"Yep. But he won't ring that number again. I've also gone ahead and put taps on Helen Tolsten's telephone and Wilbur Shearing's private number."

"They know they're on?"

Bourke prefaced his answer with a yawn. He rubbed his eyes, saying, "Of course not . . . but everything at our end's been done aboveboard. If we get anything it'll be admissible."

Carol stifled a matching yawn, stretched, and thought longingly of Sybil and home.

Bourke handed her the list of names he had read to her that morning on the phone. It itemized the

127

people who had worked for Wilbur Shearing's television channel and had then transferred to his movie interests and the set of *Death Down Under*. Typically, he had neatly written them in alphabetical order: Vic Carbond; Charlie Date; Alice Fleming; Luke West. Separately he had noted that Madeline Shipley was involved in the development of a crime series that was to include footage from the movie and that Malcolm Murtry had appeared as an actor in several programs on the channel.

"It's only preliminary stuff," he said, "but we both know quite a bit about Vic Carbond — he's skated close to the wind a number of times, mainly on morals charges, but never been convicted. The others are still being followed up and I've got a team checking their alibis for Tuesday night when Alissa Harvey was killed. It was early filming that day and so they broke up around five."

He briefly outlined general background information. Charlie Date had several convictions for drunken driving and one for failing to stop after an accident and subsequently resisting arrest. He had lost his driving license for twelve months and paid a series of hefty fines. This seemed to have sobered him somewhat; over the last year he had been clean.

Bourke said, "The psychological profile mentioned a psychopath might have a record of minor offenses."

"But did these episodes of drunken driving correspond to his marriage break-up? Alice Fleming's story is that Charlie Date's wife left him for another woman. Did you get anything on that?"

"Not a thing. Could be a reason to have a grudge

against women in general, I suppose. No use asking him — I'll get hold of his wife."

Alice Fleming seemed quite above board. She was married to a clerk in the public service and had worked in the entertainment industry for over fifteen years. "She's a gossip," he said. "Not a vicious one, but enthusiastic, so she's not the sort to let the truth get in the way of a good story." He grinned. "She's also a grandmother, so it'd be great for the media if she turns out to be the Orange Strangler. Just think of the headlines! For example, KILLER GRANNY leaps to mind."

"I always thought your unique talents are wasted in this job," Carol said dryly, "but before you apply for a position on *The Shipley Report* I'd appreciate any other information you have so far."

Luke West had been brought up by an aunt and her husband after his parents died. He had been briefly married to a girl with whom he had gone to school. "Boy next door stuff," said Bourke, "and it didn't work out. No kids to complicate the divorce, which, incidentally, took place some years after they separated. She initiated it when she met someone else she wanted to marry." Apart from several speeding fines and some parking offenses, Luke had no record of any wrongdoing.

Carol took the files from him. "How about the Fernandez case?" she asked.

"No progress yet. And I haven't got the background on Paul Crusoe either. It *is* the weekend, Carol."

She made a face. "Mark, I know how much work

this is. Tomorrow — it's my son's tenth birthday. I'll be seeing him in the morning and taking him to lunch. Then I'll come in during the afternoon."

"Think you're indispensable, do you? Carol, we don't need you till Monday. Take the whole day. Have it on me."

She smiled at him across the neat piles of documents covering his desk. "You think our Orange Strangler will continue to take weekends off too?"

"Of course. The best publicity's mid-week anyway . . . and our boy just loves publicity."

The light was beginning to fade as Carol arrived home. The house was silent and aloof. She received an offhand greeting from Sinker in the front garden and none at all from Jeffrey, who was draped on a stone step some way down the slope at the back of the house and didn't deign to lift his head when she came out onto the wide wooden deck above him. She said to him sourly, "It's quite obvious you two furry parasites have just lately been fed."

Sybil had left a note: *Gone to the beach. Back soon.*

Carol flicked at the edge of the paper, pensive. Sybil was always drawn to the sea when she was troubled. She was a strong swimmer, and would plunge into the surf even when the waves were ferocious.

Carol felt both guilty and resentful. Why hadn't Sybil warned her that Madeline knew something

130

about their relationship? During the day they had been near each other several times on the catamaran, but had behaved as strangers. But of course, that was just as they had agreed . . . or rather, she had to admit, it was as she herself had dictated.

She knew Sybil was dissatisfied with the secrecy of their relationship. "It's not," Sybil had said, "that I intend to stop strangers in the street, or run down the middle of the road with a placard. I don't want to make life difficult for you, or, for that matter, for myself. Just a little bit of low-key honesty. But you won't even discuss the matter, will you?"

And, of course, she hadn't. She avoided the issue, as she always had in the past. She had put it in the too hard basket and ignored it, letting it lie there, unresolved.

Once, smarting from a comment, she had said, "It's easy for you, Sybil, isn't it? You aren't on public display. You don't deal with people every day who'd like nothing better than to get an angle they can use against you."

Sybil's retort had seemed simplistic. "They can only use it if you let them know it's important to you by trying to hide it."

"I don't hide it. I ignore it."

After these clashes Sybil would withdraw, her laughter and tenderness armored over by a politely cool indifference that angered Carol more than direct conflict ever could.

The demanding ring of the telephone interrupted her prickly thoughts.

"Carol? It's Madeline. I need to see you — it's important."

Carol's hand trembled with a rush of boiling anger. "You demand and I jump. Is that it?"

Madeline's voice held a note of protest. "Carol, you've got it wrong. I'm no threat to you."

Feeling suddenly tired and defeated, Carol said, "I can't see you until Monday. If it's about the case, Mark Bourke's available tomorrow, or you can tell me now, on the phone."

"Carol, I really need to see you face to face. Have you got any time tomorrow?"

Madeline's voice was persuasive, coaxing. Carol set her jaw. The sooner she faced Madeline the sooner she would know what action, if any, Madeline intended to take. "I'm taking my son out tomorrow for his birthday. I'll call in to see you after I drop him home — about five in the afternoon."

After she had replaced the receiver Carol opened her briefcase and took out the folders she had brought home to look through. The information on Madeline Shipley largely consisted of career details. She had begun as a print journalist, moving on to radio and then television. Her potent combination of good looks, ambition, and talent had ensured her success in the visual medium. Two years ago she had taken a gamble, switching from a safe position as a reporter on a high-rating current affairs program to Wilbur Shearing's channel, where she was given the opportunity to build an audience with *The Shipley Report*. She had done this so successfully that Pierre Brand, formerly the undisputed leader in this prime time slot, was struggling to keep up. There was little in the report about Madeline's life outside her career. Shearing paid his extremely successful stars well, so financially she was very secure. She had been married to Paul Crusoe for five years and their partnership seemed to be a happy one, with no rumors of infidelity.

Paul Crusoe's file had more revealing information. After juvenile convictions for vandalism and car stealing, Crusoe had been arrested on two occasions for minor drug offenses, being put on a bond each time. He had been in severe financial difficulties when he had married Madeline Shipley. She had cancelled his debts and established an account for him, into which she paid a regular allowance. Although he continued to paint, and, with his wife's financial support, to exhibit, critical acclaim as an artist eluded him.

When she had seen Madeline and Paul together, Carol had thought they had an easy affection for each other. Even so, she wondered why Madeline was content with a failure like Paul. But then, Carol thought, Paul was no competition — Madeline was manifestly successful, and perhaps she preferred her partner to be dependent upon her.

It was completely dark when Carol heard Sybil's car. Armed with aggrieved worry, she opened the front door abruptly.

Sybil's red hair was wet, her color high. She kissed Carol's cheek briefly. "Hi. Let's ring for a pizza."

Carol followed her slim figure, saying without inflection, "I've been worried about you, swimming near dark. You could drown and who would know?"

"I'm careful."

"Why didn't you wait for me? I'd have gone with you."

Sybil flopped into a chair, determinedly casual. "Didn't know what time you'd be home."

Carol said flatly, "Madeline spoke to you."

Looking up at her, almost defiantly, Sybil said, "I didn't know whether to warn you or not . . . I decided you could handle it."

"Thanks."

"Don't be angry with me, Carol. You're the one who wants the secrecy, not me."

"I explained why it was necessary," Carol snapped.

Sybil looked at her steadily. "You're ashamed of me, Carol. I know you are."

"That's not true."

Standing up, Sybil said, "And you don't want to discuss it and you don't want to change. That leaves me only two options and I don't like either of them."

Carol was silent. After all, what was there to say that hadn't already been said?

Carol enjoyed her Sunday at Darling Harbour with David. She resisted wearing clothes that would suit her meeting with Madeline later in the day, relaxing instead in jeans and a tangerine sloppy joe. Sybil didn't accompany them, but sent a present and an excuse. Carol was relieved to concentrate on something and someone outside both her work and her home life. She delighted in her son's uncomplicated high spirits as they rode the monorail, purchased a stockman's hat for him, ate deliciously unhealthy food and tramped through the interactive technology displays in the Power House Museum.

She smiled at his blond head indulgently, finding herself fondly imagining him a famous scientist. Then she mocked herself for her optimistically conventional vision. Didn't all parents see their offspring as world-beaters?

Her smile faded as images of the abuse she had seen inflicted upon children rose in her mind. She swept the pictures away.

I've been too long a cop, she thought.

She watched David pushing buttons at a display and thought of last night. Suddenly and disconcertingly despairing, she'd said to Sybil, "Would you ever leave me?"

Sybil's words had burned. "You're full of questions, Carol. You ask me if I love you. You ask me if I'll leave you. But you'll never be satisfied with the answers, because of what makes you ask those questions in the first place."

"I don't understand."

Sybil had been openly scornful. "Of course you understand. The problem is, you don't want to." Glaring at Carol, she added, "Why in the hell do you think I stay with you? What's in it for me, Carol?"

Carol had kept her tone light as she had given an exaggerated shrug to embroider her words. "You stay with me because you love me and you know you could never leave me."

"You hope," Sybil had said.

Madeline had obviously been waiting for her, as she opened the door before Carol could ring the bell. She was wearing tailored dark pants and a cream-colored shirt. Without high heels she seemed diminished, both in height and personality. "We're alone — Paul's out."

Following her down the hall, Carol thought Madeline looked nervous and on edge, but had to admit that it was likely she was seeing in Madeline what she felt in herself. Madeline didn't offer refreshments, but took Carol straight to her study, closing the door firmly behind them.

Carol was ready to use reason, arguments, even threats. In her imagination she had gone over possible scenarios, played out different scenes. She sat erect, waiting for Madeline to make her first move.

Madeline seemed fully as tense as she, sitting behind her big desk, biting her lip. She used both hands to push her long copper hair back from her face, saying, "Carol, you're not going to believe me, but I know exactly how you feel."

"How could you?"

Madeline half-smiled at Carol's scorn. "I know because . . ." She took a deep breath. ". . . I'm a lesbian, too."

The word seemed to hang in the air between them. Carol always found the word fascinating, disturbing — a word to jolt her attention — a word to be avoided.

Carol thought, Would Madeline lie to disarm me?

Madeline was watching her with wide gray eyes, seeming to read her thoughts. "It's true, Carol, and I hide it, just like you. I think, I *know*, that if the public knew I was gay, I could kiss goodbye to my career. It isn't fair — but that's the way it is." She leaned forward. "And that's why," she said earnestly, "there's no way you need to worry about what I know."

"Your marriage?"

"I've known Paul a long time. We're friends, companions. It was a bargain between us, and we've both lived up to our parts: he gives me respectability, I give him financial support."

Carol sat silent, frowning. She felt a confusion of suspicion, relief, and astonishment. Her thoughts, opinions, were realigning in the light of Madeline's extraordinary confession. She said, "Paul — is he gay?"

"No. But he's one of those people — not as rare as you might think — who isn't particularly interested in sex. We have no physical relationship, of course, and whatever he may do, as long as he's discreet, is his affair."

The security of being in control was beginning to seep back for Carol. She said, "And you, Madeline, what do you do?"

Madeline's laugh held little amusement. "Me? Not much." She grew serious. "There was a woman — Ann. She was special to me, but not as important as my career. I was paranoid about bad publicity, and when it got too difficult, we broke up. Now . . . I try not to think about it too much." Grief washed across her face. She wiped it away, stood, said, "I could use a stiff drink, how about you?"

Carol felt as though she had been holding her breath since she had entered the house. She sighed as she allowed herself to relax. "Madeline — to tell me — that must have been hard."

Smiling, Madeline said, "Bloody impossible."

Chapter 10

On Monday mornings everyone around Sydney seemed to leap into the nearest vehicle and set off in thick streams to enter the city. Carol was later than usual, and paid for it by the volume of other cars competing for her position on the road, but she hardly noticed the traffic's fitful stops and starts as she turned over in her mind all the implications of Madeline's revelation. She had told Sybil what Madeline had said, but they hadn't discussed it at length. Carol was keenly aware that there were uncomfortable parallels between Madeline's life and hers, but, she assured herself, if it came to the crunch, she would never be willing to sacrifice Sybil for her career. She felt a shiver of alarm. If it came to the crunch . . .

Carol joined Bourke in his office as Mrs. Date was shown in. She was an angular woman in her early thirties with a sweet set to her mouth and a lilting voice. After a few minutes Carol had the extraneous thought that perhaps Vera Date would prefer to sing her answers to a musical accompaniment, so rhythmic was her intonation.

She positively trilled when Bourke delicately approached the story that she had left Charlie Date for another woman. "Oh, no, Detective Bourke! Indeed not. When I left Charlie I went to my best friend's place certainly, Babs Dehuntley, but there was nothing, nothing of that sort of thing."

Carol smiled at her. "Perhaps you could help us. How could such a story get around? Would it just be idle gossip?"

"Oh, no, not just gossip, bad though that can be. I'd blame Charlie for it. He probably told people that's what happened. He was always jealous of Babs. We got on so well, you know. Best friends from school. We share everything."

Bourke said, "Your friend Babs Dehuntley is married?"

Mrs. Date looked somber. Babs had been engaged to a man who had died in the war in Vietnam. She'd never found anyone else. Such a waste . . .

Pressed to discuss her husband (they would be finally and irrevocably divorced within two months) Vera Date described him as a difficult person, moody and rather selfish. "Always been that way," she said, "and frankly, I blame his mother. He was the only boy in the family and she spoiled him rotten. Charlie and I married very young — too young if you ask me — and I could put up with his behavior when the kids were growing up, but now I don't see why I should. Do you?"

Apparently not requiring an answer, she said to Bourke, "Do you think Charlie might know something about the Orange Strangler? Is that it?" She flicked a look at Carol. "And you'll be wanting to solve it quick smart, won't you, before he does another one in."

"We were actually wondering," said Carol, "whether Charlie could *be* the Orange Strangler."

Vera Date pursed her sweet mouth. "No way," she said decisively. Bourke looked questioning. She responded. "Charlie might not be the easiest man to live with, but one thing I can say about him — he's kind to animals, to living things. He wouldn't hurt anything or anybody. I even had to kill insects for him because he refused to use a spray. So you see there's no way he'd go around murdering girls the way the one you're looking for does."

Bourke continued to ask mild questions to which Mrs. Date responded freely, and when she left, apologizing for wasting their time, they had very little more information.

"Don't be too discouraged," said Carol, her bantering tone intended to lighten Bourke's gloomy expression. "It's probably no one we're investigating. Out there in suburbia our anonymous strangler waits, secure that we're tied up following false leads."

Bourke shook his head stubbornly. "No, Carol. It's someone we've come across. These links to Wilbur

Shearing's company can't just be coincidence. He, or she, is close. Sure of it."

"If we knew why . . ."

He was equally stubborn over this. "It doesn't matter *why* . . . I really don't think the motive is going to help us much, because it's personal."

"That's why it might."

"So he hates women. I don't like to denigrate my own sex, but plenty of men dislike women, and vice versa, I'm sure. And these people don't go round disposing of the hated opposite sex. They just bitch about them . . . and that's all they do."

Carol said, "What if it isn't a simplistic hatred of women? What if it's something else?"

"What — religion? I've got people checking out every way-out faith in town. Even followed up the suggestion it might be devil worship. So far everything's drawn a blank."

Showing uncharacteristic impatience, he stood and began to pace the narrow confines of his office. "Four women, and he apparently selects them at random. But three have something to do with Shearing Media — Maria Kelly acts in a pilot program, Sally-Jean Cross is romantically involved with Wilbur himself and after she's dumped gets ready to appear on *The Shipley Report,* Alissa Harvey visits the channel at least once, since she has a photograph she took on Madeline Shipley's set. Frankly, Carol, I don't believe in that much coincidence. I think we're going to find that Narelle Dent had something to do with the channel as well."

"If that's the case, it could be anyone on the staff."

He nodded, his good humor surfacing. "Yep. How

do you think we'd go asking for a voluntary blood sample from every employee for DNA profiling?"

He smiled at her expression. "True," he said quite cheerfully. "It's not the legality of it all, it's the cost, Carol, the cost! We'll need a lot more evidence before we can justify that expense, won't we?"

The day became irritating, full of inconclusive facts, fruitless telephone calls and constant interruptions. Carol and Bourke discussed the Fernandez case with the detectives involved in the original investigation and with the Crown Prosecutor's Office, but nothing of any worth emerged from the effort.

Bourke delivered a written report on Madeline Shipley's staff which contained little of interest except that Charlie Date had been assigned for six months to assist with the logistics of outside broadcasts for *The Shipley Report*, leaving the post to take over as unit manager on *Death Down Under*.

Bourke had written a note at the bottom: *Carol, how come we haven't considered Helen Tolsten as a suspect? Her life is so blameless I find that suspicious in itself.*

Carol added this report to the growing pile on her desk. It was now early evening and she felt she wanted to escape from the endless sheets of paper containing myriads of facts, most of which would turn out to be worthless. The problem, she thought wryly, had to do with perspective — a way of looking at the sea of information, an angle that could throw an unsuspected pattern into focus.

143

She decided to wait for Ferguson to deliver his report on the photographs in Alissa Harvey's camera, so she rang Sybil to explain she would be held up, then switched on the television set in her office, flicking from station to station to catch the newscasts. The Orange Strangler story was slowly sinking from sight, being forced out by newer, even if not more sensational, items.

Her attention was suddenly caught by a promo in a commercial break: "And don't miss *The Shipley Report,* right after our all-state weather. The Orange Strangler is still free to kill and tonight Madeline Shipley exclusively reveals a startling new theory the police are considering in their desperate hunt for this psychopathic killer!"

A startling new theory was news to Carol; she awaited Madeline's appearance with curiosity. She inserted a blank videotape and began to record as Madeline's face appeared.

After promising fascinating revelations later in the program, Madeline efficiently ran through her other stories, which seemed to be selected to a formula. There was a consumer rip-off for the concerned purchaser, a scare story on drugs in schools for parents, and, of course, the obligatory environmental disaster item. After a bank of commercials which, Carol thought, contained the seeds of consumer rip-offs, drugs and environmental disasters in themselves, Madeline introduced the subject of the Orange Strangler.

She gave an efficient précis of the victims and the investigation so far, including a short take of Carol asking for public assistance in the apprehension of the murderer.

The camera drew even closer to Madeline's attractive face. "And now, the last victim of a maddened killer — Alissa Harvey. An ordinary girl, a gifted photographer, a beloved daughter. But is that all there is to Alissa Harvey? It is not."

Madeline looked solemn while pausing for her audience to concentrate its attention on her next words. "Alissa Harvey led a secret life. One kept hidden from her parents, from her friends. And that secret life might have been the cause of her death . . . After this message we will investigate what it is that Alissa Harvey had to conceal."

Fury blurred the block of commercials for Carol. She snatched up the phone, then slammed it down. Grimly, she watched Madeline's features reappear, listened to her regretful tone as she revealed that Alissa Harvey had been a secret lesbian who, *The Shipley Report* had been told, had had numerous liaisons through gay bars and pick-up joints.

This part of the story was illustrated by a series of unflattering shots of dingy bars and anonymous couples in various states of inebriation and affectionate fondling.

"Could this be," said Madeline, reappearing on the screen, "the key to her dreadful death? There are suggestions, not yet confirmed, that a similar link may be found in other victims' lives. Is it possible that the very lifestyle of some young women can bring them to destruction?"

Carol snatched up the phone again. "That's it!"

she said to the charming face on the screen. "Blame the victim, Madeline. You're in good company!"

Sybil opened the front door as Carol walked down the path. "Heard your car. Did you see Madeline's program?"

Carol was cool and self-contained. "Yes. And I've spoken to her." She strode through to the living room, threw her briefcase on the couch. "I need a drink."

Sybil's voice was bright with indignation. "How could she do that, when she's a lesbian herself? And the parents — they must have been appalled."

Carol sounded quite matter-of-fact. "I'm sure they were. However, Madeline explained to me the finer points of television journalism." Her voice became sarcastic as she added, "Apparently morality is a luxury. As Madeline put it, Shearing pays her to get in first and splash it big. Her personal feelings, she said, have nothing to do with it."

"Just doing her job," said Sybil scathingly.

"That's right. She even said that if she hadn't broken the story, someone else would have, and not so sympathetically."

"Then what will stop her blowing *your* cover?" Sybil demanded.

Carol's mouth tightened. "Apparently Madeline sees that as quite a different situation — we're professional women who should help each other. Besides, I've got the goods on her as well." Carol didn't add that she was beginning to suspect that Madeline, sure that a detailed police investigation ran a good chance of finding out her secret, had revealed her lesbianism to Carol to gain an advantage. Was it too cynical to suspect that Madeline might be delighted to have a Detective Inspector beholden to her?

Before she went to bed Carol leafed through Ferguson's report on the photographs developed from the roll of film in Alissa Harvey's camera.

Bourke had pinned a note to the front of the pages to say that several of Alissa's colleagues had mentioned she was excited about a project she had conceived, but she had refused to discuss what it was.

The photographs didn't seem to be associated with any one special project. Of the twelve, Ferguson had firmly identified eight, including two taken during August or early September at Shearing's television station. One was in the studio during a *Shipley Report* program and the other, as Madeline herself had said, was taken in the courtyard outside her office.

There were three photographs taken at an accident scene where two cars had had a minor collision. Ferguson had followed this up in minute detail, obviously considering this could be one way a murderer would have every reason to obtain a strange woman's name and address.

Carol smiled a little at the disappointment

contained in Ferguson's account when what looked like a promising lead turned out to be an accident involving a neighbor backing out of his driveway and hitting the vehicle driven by Alissa's mother, Mrs. Harvey, as she drove sedately down the street.

Three other photographs were of easily identifiable locations: a busy city street, the entrance gates to the television station of one of Shearing's competitors and a charming shot of a kitten attempting to catch a bird who rose in unhurried flight before its eager paws.

The four unidentified photographs were different angles of the same subject — a Federation style suburban house, substantial and garden-surrounded. Ferguson had written: *Trying real estate agents and local councils.*

Carol frowned over the photos. Why take four shots of an unremarkable house? Was it a key to her murder, or just another blind alley leading nowhere?

Carol finished cleaning her teeth as Sybil stepped out of the shower. Carol's eyes were drawn to the wet warmth of her skin beaded with water.

"Darling," she said, trying to touch her slowly.

Sybil stood relaxed in her embrace. "It's because you're angry," she observed.

Her voice muffled against Sybil's wet shoulder, she said lightly, "It's because you're irresistible."

"Carol, you always find anger a turn-on."

She tried to kiss her into silence, but Sybil turned her head away, refusing to be diverted. "Why do you find it so exciting?"

Trembling with a need that had to be satisfied, Carol protested, "Do we have to discuss it now?"

Sybil's breath had quickened, but her tone was still reasonable. "Is it because anger is an emotion close to violence? Is that it?"

Carol couldn't concentrate on anything but the wet heat that filled her. She began to lick up the drops of water, to slide her mouth over the warm skin, to provoke a nipple with circular movements of her tongue.

Sybil was half-laughing in protest as her body responded. "Don't you want a philosophical discussion?"

"I want to go to bed."

The anger that had driven Carol was defeated, spiraling away down a dark tunnel of desire. Her body locked in sensual combat with Sybil's was all that remained. Everything else — the baffling contradictions of day-to-day life — melted away in a gasping surge of passion.

But tonight nothing seemed enough to bring her to that final blending of body and spirit, where release is the flashpoint that momentarily annihilates all emotion but joy. Sybil's eager body bucked in her arms in orgasm as she strained to reach it too, but it was like the final summit of a mountain, close but unattainable.

"Carol?"

"I can't." She held Sybil's hands. "It doesn't matter. Go to sleep."

"No. Let me —"

"Don't worry. I'm tired . . ." She released her. "Sybil, I'm all right, really."

She lay, eyes open, as Sybil curled around her.

After a while Sybil's breathing deepened as she sank into sleep, but such an escape eluded Carol. The ache between her legs slowly faded as the bleak night settled down.

Chapter 11

The morning paper was reasonably restrained. LESBIAN LINK TO SERIAL KILLER? it questioned, following this with a sketchy item obviously cobbled together in haste. The concluding paragraph narrowed Carol's eyes: *As yet unconfirmed is the report that the serial killer has contacted a news personality direct* . . . There was nothing linking this to Madeline, but Carol was sure the intention was to whet the public's appetite for future revelations.

The other two morning papers she collected on the way to work were rather more shrill. One tabloid proclaimed: LESBIAN LOVER TELLS, adding underneath in slightly smaller print, MY AFFAIR WITH STRANGLER VICTIM. The double page spread inside featured photographs of Alissa Harvey and of her self-proclaimed lover ("I was one of many . . ."). Again, there was reference to a direct approach by the murderer to the media under the sub-heading STRANGLER SPEAKS?

The third newspaper, in keeping with its image, interviewed the leader of the Family First movement (GAY SIN KILLS SAYS CLERIC) who seemed delighted at the opportunity to point out that although he and his followers truly loved all gay and lesbian people, they hated the lifestyle they followed . . . a lifestyle that was not only an affront to God, but could also, he emphatically maintained, lead unbalanced individuals towards violent and sickening acts.

Inside, a columnist mused on whether men killed the women they couldn't possess. His attitude seemed to be one of sorrow, rather than anger, as if he found it personally regretful that some women insisted on maddening males by rejecting them.

She scribbled a note to remind herself to have Bourke check out the "lover" who had so avidly provided the details on Alissa Harvey.

Carol had asked for all her calls to be stopped, so she muttered impatiently when the phone rang. The switch was apologetic, but could she speak to Madeline Shipley? It was an emergency.

"Put her on. Madeline? I'm extremely busy. What is it that's so important?"

Her expression changed as she listened. She asked a few sharp questions then rang off with the instruction for Madeline to stay by the phone.

She didn't bother with the intercom, but walked rapidly down to Bourke's office.

"Mark, Madeline Shipley's just called. Her assistant, Helen, has disappeared. She was supposed to come round to Madeline's place this morning, but she didn't turn up, and when she and Paul Crusoe investigated she wasn't at home."

Bourke lounged behind his desk, grinning. "So? She's a bit chilly for my taste, but maybe she let her hair down and had a night on the town."

"Think it's more than that. Madeline told me that Helen has been lining up an exclusive interview with the Orange Strangler."

Bourke stood. "There's been nothing on the phone taps. I've just been through the transcriptions. How —"

"He made contact Sunday, on Shearing's boat. Madeline was speaking to me when Helen came up to say there was an urgent call. He could have been ringing from a car, from anywhere."

Bourke's response was instant. "Of the suspects we've got, were there any near you when the call came? Is there anyone we can rule out of contention?"

Carol recreated the scene in her imagination. "Madeline was with me when Helen came to tell her about the call. I didn't see anyone else of interest — most people had disembarked."

Bourke said, "So Helen spoke to him first, then

she came to collect Madeline. I don't suppose Helen would be fool enough to make an appointment to meet this guy herself, would she?"

"Madeline told her not to do anything dangerous or stupid, but Helen was handling the whole thing and kept her in the dark."

His tone scathing, Bourke said, "Madeline's keeping her hands clean, eh? So she can't be accused of hindering the police, she makes sure she doesn't know any details." He shook his head. "Poor bloody little fool," he added angrily, obviously thinking of Helen.

Carol was eager to be doing something active. "The car Helen drives is missing and it's registered to Madeline's company. Here's the information you need. I'll leave you to handle everything here while I go to Madeline's house. You can get me there if you need me. Make sure Helen Tolsten *is* missing before you put out an all points. Cover the media — every outlet. To hell with the fact we're feeding them sensational stuff, ham it up as much as you like. I want Helen found, dead or alive, as fast as possible, and I don't care how it's done."

Madeline and Paul were standing together in Paul's untidy studio when the housekeeper showed Carol into the room. The brightly colored canvases — stacked in corners, hanging unevenly on the walls, piled negligently against the couch — provided an incongruous backdrop.

Carol had never seen Madeline in anything but the most elegant clothes, but today she was wearing a pair of old jeans and an outsize blue shirt. Her face was white and even her bright copper hair seemed to have lost its luster.

Paul Crusoe had a comforting arm around his wife's shoulders, but he himself looked quite unperturbed. He said, "Have you heard anything?"

Carol kept her tone soothing, calm. "No. Not yet. Madeline, you told me on the phone Helen was here at the house last night. Exactly what happened and when did she leave?"

Madeline's voice was husky and held none of its usual confidence. "After the show last night Helen drove me home. She often does. We got here a little after eight. Paul had waited for us and we had dinner together . . ." She bit her lip. Carol waited.

"Carol, she was so excited. We both were. An interview with the Orange Strangler . . . it was going to shoot way over Pierre Brand's ratings."

Keeping the anger out of her voice, Carol said, "Do you really think he was going to go ahead with it? Voice prints alone, quite apart from the risk of being identified any other way, should make an interview a very unattractive proposition."

Madeline shook off Paul's arm and began to pace up and down the cluttered room. Emphasis entered her voice as she defended herself. "Yes, I thought he was going to give me an interview and yes, he'd thought of all the risks. He's so conceited, Carol, so sure of himself. You can hear it in his voice. And Helen had worked it all out with him, how to electronically disguise his voice, how to protect him." She looked almost defiantly at Carol. "And of course, we were going to hand everything we got over to you . . ."

155

"After you'd telecast the interview."

"Well, yes. You'd have done the same, Carol, in my position."

Carol wondered if the disgust she felt showed on her face. She said, "Had Helen actually met him at any stage?"

"No. We agreed it was too dangerous." She looked down. "But last night . . . Helen said she was only going to talk to him again, that she had a contact number, but I didn't fully believe her. I thought . . . but I wasn't sure . . . Wouldn't have let her do it if I had been . . ."

Carol thought, You ruthless bitch, of course you would. She said, "You have the contact number? Did Helen make a recording of their conversations? Any details at all?"

Madeline moved impulsively to touch her arm. "Carol, please believe me, if I'd realized . . ." She let her hand drop. "Helen wanted to protect me. She knew we were skating close to the wind from the legal point of view, so she kept the fine details from me. I think she might have taped the calls, but she didn't say so directly. She didn't want me involved in the negotiations."

Carol's tone was caustic. "You were working on the principle of what you didn't know couldn't hurt you."

Paul filled the silence. "Helen left here between nine-thirty and ten. I came back here to paint. Madeline went to bed early. She said she was tired."

"Was your housekeeper still here?"

Madeline looked at her sharply. "What are you saying, Carol? That we, Paul and I, need an alibi?"

"I'm saying that details like this are just for the record. Nothing more."

"And nothing less," added Paul. He raised his eyebrows. "Aren't you jumping the gun a bit, Inspector? After all, we don't know that an alibi's necessary at all. Helen might have just taken off somewhere."

Carol ignored the comment, repeating her query about the housekeeper.

"She served the meal to us and went to her rooms. Edna has a self-contained flat attached to the house."

"I'd like to see her, if that's all right."

Madeline's momentary energy had dissipated. She sank onto the couch, pushing a leaning canvas over as she did so. Bending slowly to pick it up, Paul said, "Hope it's not an omen, what you just did."

"What?"

"This canvas, Madeline. It's of Helen. I was doing her portrait, remember?"

Carol was intrigued, moving till she could see the painting. She was surprised at how well he had caught the likeness. It was half-finished, but recognizably Helen Tolsten. She stared arrogantly from the orange background of the canvas, neck stiff with self-satisfaction.

Paul Crusoe showed relaxed amusement at her interest. "You see, Inspector," he said, "there's no way I would kill Helen. The artist in me wouldn't allow it — not until I'd finished her portrait at any rate."

Carol continued her questions, finding out that the call to Shearing's catamaran had been about the program Madeline was preparing on the Orange Strangler. "So the arrangements Helen was making were concerned with this personal interview with him that was to be incorporated into the program?"

Madeline wearily covered her eyes with one hand. "Yes."

Impatient and angry, but keeping her voice mild, Carol asked to see Edna. She interviewed her in the kitchen and, having completed her questions, was being shown out by Madeline and Paul.

Madeline had begun to say, "Paul, would you contact Wilbur and say I can't go on tonight. It's absolutely —" The telephone interrupted her, and she stood, apprehensive, while Edna answered it.

"Inspector Ashton, it's for you."

"Yes?" She listened, tight-mouthed. "Where exactly? I'll meet you there. I'm leaving now."

She hung up, stood looking at the floor for a moment, then turned to their waiting eyes. "I'm sorry, Madeline."

"Helen . . ."

"We think we've found her body."

"Was it —"

Carol's voice was bitter with anger. "The Orange Strangler, Madeline? Indeed it was. Under the circumstances, how could you doubt it?"

The grass was newly mowed and a sprightly green. The stream that ran through Parramatta Park was no doubt polluted, but it still sparkled fetchingly in the glare of sunlight. The nearby footbridge crossed the glinting water at the foot of the rise that held the historic bulk of Old Government House. A knot of people, enclosed by blue and white fluttering tapes, were engrossed with something lying on the scented grass beneath a clump of bushes.

Uniformed police officers were busy with crowd control as Carol drew into the car park which was usually filled with tourist buses. She called the sergeant in charge over to her car. "Keep everybody back. Everybody. But I want you and the others to look at them carefully. Memorize their faces. It's not unknown for a murderer to join the people who collect around a crime scene. And this one's a psycho. He, or she, is unlikely to show nervousness or alarm — will probably look just like an ordinary person. Even so, if there's anything unusual at all, tell me about it."

As she spoke she scanned the crowd herself, hearing the excited voices and speculation. "It's him again, the strangler!" someone was saying loudly with impressive accuracy. Was anyone there familiar to her? Or was a person, recognizing her, even now walking quickly away?

Bourke raised a hand to her and she began to make her way quickly down the grassy slope even though she was filled with a shrinking reluctance to see Helen Tolsten's confidence reduced to the indignity of such a death.

Bourke moved to stand beside her. "Looks like it's her — the driver's license and other papers match. You've seen her several times, Carol. What do you think?"

The scientific squad had tied back the branches of the bushes and the sunlight dappled the naked body in shifting patterns. It was laid out in the same way as the other four victims, in parody of mourning, the orange cord at her feet and hands a cheery color against the paleness of the skin.

Carol's voice was cool. "The build's right. Can we take the pillowcase off yet?"

Bourke gestured to one of the technicians to remove the white covering that swathed the head, saying, "Yes, they've done all they can here. We were waiting for you to see the body before we moved it."

They looked down at Helen Tolsten's face. "Jesus," said Bourke under his breath, then louder, to Carol, "I think it's her. You agree?"

"Yes, Mark, it's Helen Tolsten. We've got to move fast. This time we've got suspects to follow up."

He gave her a muted version of his normal cheeky grin. "How you doubt me," he said. "As we speak, the wheels are in motion. By the time we get back to headquarters the preliminary reports should be coming in."

Chapter 12

Death Down Under's second last day of location shooting in Sydney was at Harold Park Trotting Track. Sybil had both Malcolm and Kirra seated at the cramped caravan table struggling with schoolwork when Charlie Date put his head through the doorway. Malcolm looked up, delighted to be interrupted; Kirra ploughed on, tongue firmly placed in the corner of her mouth, forehead wrinkled with concentration.

"Meeting's been called," he said. "The whole crew, right now, down by the catering truck." He frowned at Malcolm and Kirra. "You two kids as well. Hurry up. It's urgent."

"What's it all about?"

Charlie was aggravated by Malcolm's question. "Dunno. Come on, hop to it."

He was more forthcoming to Sybil as they walked past the stands and towards the rapidly growing group of restive people. His tone was pleasant but concerned as he said, "Something's up, Syb. It's the cops. Wanted a copy of yesterday and today's Call Sheet and they've upset Ripley by taking over his trailer for interviews. What you think it is, uh?"

She was saved from confessing her ignorance by an excited Alice, bubbling with information. "Just heard the news flash on the radio! It's absolutely horrible! He's killed another one — the Orange Strangler has."

Charlie abruptly stopped walking. "So is that why the cops are here? Do they think —"

Alice finished his sentence. "That one of us is the strangler!" She looked around avidly. "Who? Who could it be? Are they picking on any one person? Who do you think it is?"

Charlie glowered at her. "It could be you, Alice. Why not? Doesn't have to be a man. Maybe you get your kicks that way, killing girls."

Flushed with indignation, Alice turned on him. "That's bloody nonsense! How could you say that?"

"You've been saying that, and worse, about me. I've heard you, don't think I haven't." He paused, then added as an afterthought, "You bitch."

Any possible rejoinder from Alice was cut off by a police officer, who had come to chivvy them towards the meeting. As the three of them stopped at the

162

edge of the crowd, Sybil recognized Wilbur Shearing's tight curly hair, bull neck and stocky shape.

She was standing directly behind Luke, and since they were of similar height, she could clearly see his pink scalp showing through his thinning fair hair. He turned around as though he felt her eyes upon him. His lean face lit by a smile, he said, "Hey, Syb, what have you done, that the police have called us all together?"

Alice's manner was heavy with portent. "We think it's because someone here is a suspect for the stranglings . . . there's been another one, you know."

"Has there? Where? Near here?"

Alice shook her head, obviously pleased to be the source of information. "No. Parramatta. Parramatta Park, actually. Must have done it last night. Wonder who she was."

"No one we know. Just some unlucky girl," said Charlie firmly.

Malcolm, who had sidled up to listen, said, "Picks them for a reason. Bet this one's a leso, too."

Sybil was suddenly so full of rage she could have struck him.

Charlie spoke before she could say or do anything. "You stupid little prick," he said contemptuously, "what would you know?"

Wilbur Shearing had climbed onto the back of the catering trailer. He began to speak in his staccato voice and everyone fell silent. His message was brief and to the point. The police were investigating a murder. They had reason to suppose some people here might be able to help their inquiries. He was sure that every person would cooperate fully with the police in the performance of their duties.

"Bloody cops," said Vic Carbond to Sybil, who had moved away from the antagonism that had flared between Charlie and Malcolm.

She amused herself by imagining what Carbond would say if he knew Inspector Carol Ashton was her lover. "You don't like the police?" she inquired.

He shrugged. "They're bloody stupid — most of them," he said. "Bunch of officious bastards — and half of them on the take."

"Mr. Carbond?" said an official voice. "Would you mind coming this way, sir?"

Bourke said from the doorway of Carol's office, "Helen Tolsten's car's been found."

Carol looked up from the notes she was reading. "Where?"

"In the channel's car park. She went back there after leaving Madeline Shipley and her husband."

She gestured for him to sit down. "Could someone else have driven the car?"

He moved a pile of folders from the chair and placed them neatly on the stack in Carol's in-tray. "It's possible. Staff members are required to have a sticker on their cars or they don't get entry. Besides checking that the sticker's current, the guy on the gate is supposed to record registration numbers and times. In reality, what he does is to wave through anyone who looks official, and to hell with rego numbers and the like."

"So Helen's car could have been put there at any time."

"The television station broadcasts twenty-four

164

hours a day, so there's activity most of the time. Mind you, he does say he remembers Helen driving in about ten-thirty."

Carol leaned back and surveyed him thoughtfully. "You don't sound very convinced."

"I don't think we can rely much on what he says. It's hardly a riveting job, he's not the brightest boy on the block and he's got the distraction of a portable television set in his little command post. She could have come in earlier and been killed in the car park. What I do know is she didn't sign to go into the building, and that does seem to be policed pretty well by security." He handed her a photostat sheet. "Here's a copy of security's register for last night. Looks straightforward."

Carol took it absently. "So Helen may have met someone in the car park. No doubt it's too much to hope the guard remembers her leaving, either on foot or in a car with someone else?"

"Far too much to hope for, Carol. Seems he devotes what little attention he has to the vehicles entering the car park. Those leaving probably don't even get a cursory glance."

Carol played with her black opal ring. Bourke said, "I've moved heaven and earth. The post mortem's underway right now and I'll get the report to you as soon as I can."

Carol nodded wearily and, after a moment, Bourke said, "You realize he's done the western suburbs now . . . as though he's determined to cover each broad area of the city."

"Even if that's true, it doesn't help us much, if at all."

"And," said Bourke, "he's inconsiderately

165

destroyed one of my pet theories. Remember I said he'd have to select a victim from one of the other main religions? Well, he's blown it by doubling up on Catholics. Makes you wonder who you can rely on, Carol. It really does."

"Syb, the cops asked me where I was last night. Wanted all the details," said Malcolm with some satisfaction.

Kirra was obviously suffering from chagrin. "They didn't ask me anything at all. Not a single thing."

"That's because you're just a kid. You wouldn't be any help at all."

"Were *you* a help?" asked Sybil without apparent guile.

While he was considering a reply, Kirra regarded him thoughtfully. She said, "Do they think you're the Orange Strangler?"

"Of course they don't!"

"Then why bother asking you questions?"

"You wouldn't understand," he said loftily. To Sybil he added, "Got to go through my lines for the next scene with Amy. Sorry I can't finish the lesson."

Kirra waited until he had left the caravan before she said, "He isn't, you know . . . sorry, I mean."

Sybil smiled at her automatically, all the while fitting the role of murderer to Malcolm's handsome teen-age self. He was tall and strong and she could picture with disturbing clarity his large tanned hands using a length of brightly colored cord to throttle the life out of a struggling woman.

166

* * * * *

This time Bourke came into Carol's office and sat down. "What time did Paul, Madeline and the victim eat dinner last night?"

Carol thought how angry Helen Tolsten would have been to be relegated to the role of victim. She looked at the notes she had made while speaking to Edna. "Eight-thirty to nine. Then the housekeeper loaded the dishwasher, said goodnight and left them."

Bourke handed her several stapled sheets. "Here's the post mortem report and it confirms she died in the evening. Digestion of the meal indicates she was dead within an hour of eating it . . . at the outside, an hour and a half."

"An hour? Paul Crusoe said she left between nine-thirty and ten. If she finished eating at nine, that doesn't give much time for her to meet someone somewhere else."

Bourke looked pleased. "It doesn't does it? Almost looks as if La Shipley and Paul could have combined to dispatch her."

Carol raised her eyebrows. "You see them working as a team to kill Madeline's personal assistant? It's too close to home and they're not that stupid."

Leaning his elbow on the edge of her desk, he said persuasively, "It could be one or the other working alone. You said neither had an alibi — Madeline says she went to bed and straight to sleep, Paul says he painted, though why in the hell he'd do that under artificial light I can't imagine."

Carol, who was finding she disliked Paul's paintings almost as much as she did his person,

167

struggled to be fair. "There must be a lot an artist can do without natural light . . . roughing out scenes, blocking figures — that sort of thing."

Bourke grinned. "How about artistically blotting out Helen Tolsten's life? Wouldn't it be easy to say goodbye like the perfect host, kiss your wife goodnight, then follow Helen outside where she's getting into her car, kill her and hide her body for later disposal."

"Why drive her car to the channel's car park?"

"To make it seem she's had the opportunity to meet her killer there."

"The person who dumped her car would be on foot. How does he or she get away? Walk?"

"Checking the taxis," said Bourke, "but my favorite scenario has Madeline Shipley in her car waiting for Paul outside the channel. How do you like it?"

"Not much," said Carol.

Chapter 13

Helen Tolsten's body had been found that morning but it already seemed to Carol that this event had occurred some time ago. The day had passed in a blur of activity — her telephone rang constantly, disparate pieces of information flooded in from the detectives assigned to different areas of the investigation, the Commissioner paid a personal visit and mentioned casually that his friend, Wilbur Shearing, was requesting an urgent meeting and would be in about four. Would that be all right?

Shearing was escorted to Carol's office by a young

officer who looked sideways at him with wary interest as she opened the door for him. He flashed the officer a smile, turning it off immediately as he focused his complete attention on Carol.

"I know how busy you are, Inspector. Sorry, but I had to insist on seeing you. Helen Tolsten's death . . ."

Carol studied him as she gestured for him to take a seat. His monumental self-assurance seemed a little dented by this latest murder. He swallowed nervously several times and moved his heavy shoulders uneasily as he sat. She leaned forward, all attention and interest, and waited.

Shearing cleared his throat, turning his head on his thick neck as though to ease tension. "Inspector, I'm afraid I haven't been altogether frank with you . . ."

Carol essayed mild surprise, but remained silent.

"The fact is . . . I suppose you've found out already . . ."

He waited for confirmation. Carol looked encouraging.

Shearing forced himself to lean back in his chair. He said rapidly, "I did go out once with Maria Kelly. I'm sure you know that already. There was nothing to it. She was an attractive girl. I met her during the shooting of a pilot program . . ."

Carol had maintained an interested expression, surprised though she was at the mention of the Orange Strangler's first victim and Wilbur Shearing's association with her. She said without accusation, "You denied knowing her at all when I asked you during our first interview."

"Inspector, you know how it is. I couldn't help

170

you in any way. There was nothing to it — just a casual date."

Making it a statement, not a question, she said, "This was shortly before Maria Kelly was murdered."

He winced at the slight emphasis she gave to the last word. "Yes. I was horrified, of course, but there was nothing I could do — she was dead, and frankly, I didn't want to be involved. You can imagine what a beat-up that sort of story would get in the media."

Carol thought of all the ordinary people whose tragedies had been plundered to supply material to his media empire for the edification and entertainment of the general public. The irony in her voice was clear as she said, "It was important for you to protect your privacy?"

He seemed impervious to any implied criticism. "That's why I thought it best to make a clean breast of things. I wouldn't welcome any publicity."

Puzzled, she said, "But why would there be any? Helen Tolsten's death will be the focus of attention."

His expression changed. As he licked his lips, Carol said, "You went out with Helen Tolsten too?"

"Well, yes, in a manner of speaking. Nothing serious, but when I heard how she had died, I saw at once how it would look, so I came to you immediately. I don't want you wasting your time following red herrings."

She smiled briefly at him. "You being the red herring in question?"

"Inspector, I don't find this at all amusing."

Carol stood. "Nor do I, Mr. Shearing. Could you tell me where you were last night?"

"You're not trying to accuse me . . ."

"It would be helpful if you would cooperate."

"I was alone most of the time. Had something to eat at my usual restaurant — they'll remember me — and then went home."

"What time would you have left the restaurant?"

He ran a hand over his tightly curled hair. "Not sure. Probably about nine-thirty, or maybe a bit later."

Carol looked at him steadily and he returned her gaze with an almost arrogant stare. She said, "I'll arrange for you to make a full statement. We will require dates, times and places. And confirmation of every detail."

"I want your guarantee there'll be no leak to reporters."

She hid her scorn, saying coolly, "You would know better than I that that's an impossible thing to guarantee."

Handing Shearing's statement to Bourke, Carol said, "I want to know if this is true in every detail. He may be playing frank and open, hoping that we won't look any deeper."

Bourke read swiftly through the document. He pursed his lips. "I suppose he could be the strangler, but I'm beginning to think it's less and less likely. Wilbur Shearing as the killer of five women just doesn't seem to fit, especially as Helen Tolsten's so close to home. You'd think he'd avoid making a victim of someone he'd openly taken out." He frowned. "What in the hell would someone like Shearing see in Helen Tolsten anyway?"

"Perhaps there were mutual advantages."

172

"Such as?"

"That's what I'd like you to find out." She began to doodle arrows and circles down the margin of a page. She said, "What if this is the first one that *isn't* the serial killer? What if Helen Tolsten's murder is deliberately a copycat?"

Bourke shook his head, unconvinced. "It's too good a copy. Quite apart from the use of identical orange rope, lividity shows Helen was, like all the others, killed in one place and then hidden somewhere for a while before being taken to Parramatta Park for the final ritual laying out."

Carol threw her pen down. "So it's the same person — and he's not going to stop at five."

"Why should he?" said Bourke, "since he thinks he's invincible, and we haven't done anything to prove him wrong."

Carol tossed her car keys on the kitchen counter. "Where are you?" she called, suddenly anxious.

"Here, in the second bedroom. I'm packing. We leave for Ayers Rock the day after tomorrow."

"I'm lost in admiration at your efficiency," said Carol as she kissed her lightly. She changed into jeans and a shirt and came back to say, "Mark and I will be on the set tomorrow to speak to a couple of people."

Sybil looked up from her packing. "No doubt I'm to pretend I've never seen you before?"

"It's to protect you . . . just in case."

Sybil was offhand. "If you say so."

Standing in the doorway watching Sybil expertly

173

fold and pack clothes, Carol was reminded of Bourke's comment about the strangler — *Knows how to fold things so they won't crush — neat at packing* . . .

"Sybil, do you have much to do with Alice Fleming?"

"She a suspect?"

"Could be."

Sybil turned to face her. "You're joking!"

"The clothes of each victim are folded very carefully, as though they're about to be packed into a suitcase. Everything's very neat, exact."

"Alice doesn't fit that description — at least not personally . . . she's sort of enthusiastically untidy. But as far as the clothes for the actors are concerned, well, I suppose you could say it's her job to be obsessively neat."

Carol looked pensively at the half-filled suitcase. "Is there any way you can get out of going to Ayers Rock? Do you have to be there?"

"It's in my contract, Carol. Kirra and Malcolm are in quite a few of the scenes to be shot in the Outback, so I have to be there as their tutor."

"It's just that the link between the strangler and Walter Shearing's television channel seems to be getting stronger and stronger. I'd be happier if you didn't go."

"Carol, most of the time we'll be out in the desert. Everyone knows everyone else in the crew and there'll be precious little privacy. Do you really think someone's going to plan murder in a situation like that?"

Concern made Carol's tone urgent. "You must understand he or she is a risk-taker. Psychopathic personalities don't suffer form nerves or worry like

174

we would . . . they literally can't conceive of being caught."

"And you don't have a firm suspect yet?"

"No." She watched Sybil packing shoes into the corners of the suitcase. "Darling, when you first went on to the set of *Death Down Under* did you get the impression that someone was familiar . . . that you'd seen him or her somewhere before?"

"Ripley Patterson," said Sybil promptly. "Because he's a real star," she added with a grin.

"Aside from him — someone in the crew, for example."

"I don't think so. Why?"

Carol was frowning over an elusive memory. "It's just that both Mark and I thought we saw a familiar face, but neither of us can remember who or why."

"Someone with a police record? A former lover?" said Sybil lightly.

Carol took Sybil's hand. "I love you," she said unexpectedly, surprising both of them with her sincerity.

Sybil chose to treat it lightheartedly. "Is this because I'm going away? It must be a premature case of absence making the heart grow fonder!"

Later that evening as her ancient percolator hissed and burbled fiercely, Carol perched on a high stool at the breakfast bar, wearily brooding over Bourke's neat grid setting out the whereabouts of the main suspects when Helen Tolsten was killed.

"Want a coffee?" she called to Sybil.

"No, thanks, I'm going to bed . . . are you going to be long?"

"A while."

Sybil, barefoot and in pale blue silk pajamas, came

175

to slide an arm around her waist. "Can't I tempt you?"

Carol kissed her briefly. "I really need to go through these papers."

There was a hint of protest in Sybil's voice. "We only have tonight and tomorrow night. The crew, and that includes me, flies out on Friday."

"Okay, darling. I'll try not to be too long."

She poured herself a mug of coffee and turned over the pages, forcing herself to concentrate. The post mortem had established that digestion had abruptly halted within an hour of the substantial meal Helen shared with Paul and Madeline, and this time-frame matched with the other indications of body temperature and rigor mortis. The time of death was therefore approximately ten o'clock on Tuesday night.

Carol cupped her chin with her hand as she thought. It would take at least an hour to drive to Parramatta Park, arriving at the earliest at eleven o'clock. How long would it take to strip and lay out the body? And surely the chances of unwanted witnesses would be high. It made sense to wait until the early hours of the morning, so where was Helen Tolsten's body concealed after her murder? In a car? Under one of the thick bushes that grew beside the windows of Paul Crusoe's studio? In the shadows of the television channel's car park? Or did Madeline and Paul kill her together after the housekeeper had left them for the night, leaving her body lying in a room until they moved it in the early hours of the morning?

Vic Carbond, Ripley Patterson, Luke West and Malcolm (who never missed an opportunity to see himself on the screen) had watched the rushes from Monday's scenes at the studio in Darlinghurst, leaving to go their separate ways at about nine. Vic Carbond went straight to a local pub and had been remembered unfavorably by the barmaid because he'd made a series of coarse remarks about her that had caused gales of drunken laughter from the patrons. She was unsure when he had left. He said it was well after ten-thirty.

Malcolm Murtry claimed to have caught a cab to Kings Cross, wandered alone around the fleshpots for a while, "Just for something to do . . . looking around." And then had gone home about eleven. Both his father and his brother were already in bed, so there was no corroboration of the time of his home-coming or if he went out again later.

Ripley Patterson had gone straight back to his hotel to learn his lines and have an early night. He spoke to no one and received no telephone calls.

Luke West had called on his Aunt Bea who lived alone in an inner-city terrace house, spending some time fixing a faulty light in her bathroom and leaving about a quarter to eleven.

Wilbur Shearing's story had yet to be checked, Alice Fleming had been baby-sitting her granddaughter from seven onwards, and Charlie Date had been seeing a personal counselor about his drinking and marriage problems.

Both Paul Crusoe and Madeline Shipley had been in Helen's company until shortly before her death, when Madeline claimed to have gone to bed and Paul had remained, he asserted, in his studio painting until after twelve.

It had been a pleasant spring night when Helen

Tolsten died. Bourke was hopeful that young lovers wandering through Parramatta Park might have seen something useful, but despite appeals to the public, no one had come forward with any helpful information.

There was, however, considerable unhelpful assistance, including a psychic who claimed to have foretold the murder of a woman with the initials H.T., a well-dressed and earnest former businessman who had previously confessed to most of the sensational murders of the past decade and wished to include Helen Tolsten on his list, and a convincingly down-to-earth middle-aged woman who revealed that her younger brother not only sent her a constant stream of messages through mental radio, but had also been responsible for at least two of the Orange Strangler murders — her other brother having accomplished the other three.

She pushed the papers into her briefcase and went to stand at the bedroom door. She could hear Sybil's even breathing.

"Darling, are you still awake?"

She frowned at the relief she felt when she realized Sybil was already asleep.

Chapter 14

Thursday was bright and windy. Clouds were torn to strips and the branches of the gum trees heaved and thrashed with a noise that combined the sounds of rain and of the sea.

Carol had risen at dawn and, fortified with strong coffee, had made a list of questions to which Bourke had still not provided answers.

She sat musing, watching through the glass doors the cats skittering around the wooden deck. Windy weather always made them irresponsible. Ignoring feline middle-aged spread, they stalked and pounced, playing an elaborate teasing game of kittenish tag that always ended in a spat.

Sybil came out as Carol was getting ready to leave. "Be home at a reasonable time tonight?" she said hopefully.

Carol felt a rush of tenderness. "No matter what," she said, hugging Sybil so tightly that she complained.

Early though she was to work, Bourke was there before her. He brought her a mug of coffee and perched on the edge of her desk. He ran his eyes down the list of questions she handed him. "Okay, Carol, I've got some answers for you. First, you said Malcolm Murtry saw Narelle Dent on television some time before she died. I put Ferguson on it and he says one of her friends remembers she was witness to something that made the news and she was interviewed. Don't know what it was, yet, but probably a crash or a fire or something like that. I've told him to follow it up."

Carol looked doubtfully at the contents of the mug he had given her. "Is this supposed to be coffee?"

"A near relation," said Bourke with a grin. "And the best the Department can provide." He went back to the list. "About the relationship between Shearing and Helen Tolsten — the general consensus is she was in it to help her career and he was in it for the sex. Now, about Alissa Harvey — no, she didn't do the publicity photographs for Malcolm Murtry. That was taken care of by his agent, no doubt for a kickback from the photographer."

"Have you had time to follow up the newspaper article?"

"You mean the one where her lover tells all? Charming piece of work she is. Had the pleasure of interviewing her myself last night. She was paid for the article of course, so she went along with the journalistic excesses. What I did get from her was that Alissa was working on something to do with domestic violence."

"Mark, that could tie in with the Fernandez case. I want you to go back to her parents and ask to see all her personal papers and photographs. I think they'll cooperate, but if not, get a search warrant."

"Okay. Now, about identifying the house that was on the roll of film in Alissa's camera . . . you do realize the population of Sydney's over three million?"

"Is this your indirect way of saying you haven't found it, Mark?"

"We know it's built in Federation style so it must be in one of the older suburbs, but that's as far as we've got. Ferguson's got some junior officers going from area to area showing the photos to local councils and property agents. It's taking a lot of time, and maybe Alissa just photographed it because she happened to like Federation architecture."

Carol had a sudden thought. "Sally-Jean Cross was an investigative journalist. What was she working on when she died?"

Bourke frowned. "Well, it wasn't domestic violence. Something about victims of crime and trauma counseling, I think."

"No link to Alissa Harvey? She couldn't have been providing photographs to Sally-Jean?"

"No record they ever met, though they may have, casually."

Carol was aggravated by a niggling memory that refused to come out of hiding. She tried coaxing it with concentrated thought, but it sank obstinately deeper. "Mark, both of us have a sneaking feeling there's something familiar about someone on the movie set. Don't suppose it's come to you who it is?"

"No, but it's associated with something a long time ago. I wondered if it was simply that we both remembered the face of one of the actors with a small part . . . Some of them have been on television for years."

Carol nodded and dismissed the subject, knowing it would linger just on the edge of her mind as an irritating shadow until it came out into the light.

Death Down Under was still filming at Harold Park. The stands were deserted except for the bottom tiers which were packed with extras dressed in the styles of the fifties and doing their best to look like a substantial crowd. Harness racing horses, ears pricked and feet picked up daintily, were lining up with their precariously balanced drivers for a fictitious race.

Vic Carbond was god of this particular world and was reluctant to have two police officers, however important their business, intruding on the set.

"This is the second time!" he exclaimed. "Shearing and some of your cops held us up yesterday, too. Look, I've got deadlines. We've got to be in Central Australia by the weekend. We're already over schedule and it's bloody getting hotter and hotter out there. I don't want any more interruptions."

He reluctantly released Luke West: ". . . And I'll need him in half an hour. Got that? The others — don't take them away. I want them within call."

Luke was grinning as he settled himself into a chair in Ripley Patterson's sumptuous trailer. "Poor Ripley's getting jack of being asked to shoot through every time you cops turn up," he observed.

As Bourke began to ask a series of unthreatening questions about his career with Shearing Media, Carol assessed him. He smoothed his fair hair once, then sat alert and cooperative, without seeming too eager to please.

She remembered what Sybil had said about Luke: "He's a nice guy, easy to get on with but maybe a bit empty underneath. He was the only one of the film crew who recognized me, but he was sympathetic and kept his promise not to say anything about my rather lurid past."

Carol was always interested in how a person being questioned responded to the situation. When anxious or deliberately trying to dissemble, people often gave far more information than required as though keen to cover every eventuality. Luke seemed quite relaxed, answering each question fully, but never volunteering anything additional.

Bourke apologized for going over ground that other officers had already covered, but asked him again about his alibi for the time Helen Tolsten was killed.

He repeated the information they already knew — that he had gone to his Aunt Bea's place and had replaced a faulty light switch in her bathroom.

"You left when?"

"Eleven, maybe eleven-thirty."

Carol said, "You often see your aunt?"

"Of course, she brought me up when my parents died, and now Uncle Jim's gone, I often drop in to give a hand around the place."

Bourke observed that Luke had had several convictions for speeding.

"I was a kid with a motorbike . . . did the usual stupid things." He grinned. "Drive a car now, and very sedately."

Bourke asked to examine the truck and equipment that Luke used, leaving Carol to question Alice Fleming.

Alice was obviously delighted to be interviewed. Wearing a shapeless dress of indeterminate color, her hair escaping from the rough ponytail she had secured with a thick rubber band, she settled herself down for a good gossip. "Everyone on the set talks to me," she declared, "and I'm absolutely shocked, Inspector, positively chilled, to even think that one of them could be this dreadful murderer!"

"It is disquieting," Carol agreed.

"Of course, I've had my suspicions, but nothing you could actually put your finger on, as the saying goes."

"Please tell me anything you think might be helpful."

"I don't like to name names, you understand. I mean, it's just a *suspicion* . . . a *feeling* . . ."

Carol mentally rolled her eyes in exasperation but maintained an intent, interested expression.

Alice's thin lips sucked on the name, turning it round in her mouth. Finally she expelled it. "Charlie Date!" she declared.

"You have reason to believe Charlie Date may be a murderer?"

Her mild question drew a flurry of expostulations. Alice would never, never accuse someone of murder, not even Charlie Date. He was a brutal creature, she was afraid, but every person was entitled, surely, to some element of doubt . . . However, if the Inspector were to investigate closely, she was sure something unsavory, something underhand, could be revealed . . .

Wondering if Alice had some personal grudge against Charlie Date, or if she made a habit of denigrating her colleagues in general, Carol asked Alice's opinions about others on the set. For Vic Carbond she had a few scathing remarks about his personal life, but praise for him professionally. Ripley Patterson was, in contrast, all a gentleman should be. Carol cut the rhapsodies short and asked about Malcolm Murtry.

"Malcolm?" she said scornfully. "Bit big for his boots . . . thinks himself a new James Dean. Smolders all over the place trying to look sexy . . ." She added with a shriek of laughter, "But he looks to me like his pants are too tight!"

Luke West she thought friendly, but underneath a bit standoffish. "You know," she said, "sometimes I think he deliberately avoids me. That sort of person, you know."

Carol had the wry thought that she, herself, might be "that sort of person" as far as Alice was concerned. "You've worked for Shearing Media before," she observed.

Alice, without prompting, began to discuss Wilbur Shearing. She had, she declared, regarded Sally-Jean Cross as a personal friend . . . "And Shearing treated her like dirt, you know, dropping her for that other little tramp. Of course, I've known Wilbur for years, on and off. You've got to give it to him — he knows how to make money. And he's a generous boss, I mean, *I've* got no complaints, personally, but he has enemies, plenty of them."

Carol let her talk on for a while, but she said nothing of any real interest. Carol interrupted, "You were baby-sitting on Tuesday night?"

This induced a dive into her bag and a shuffling of photographs, Alice being one of those disarming people who believe that there is no one unsusceptible to the charms of grandchildren. Smiling, Carol said, "So she's a good baby? Sleeps right through when you're looking after her."

Alice's enthusiasm abated somewhat. "Have to keep an eye on her all the time," she said. "Wouldn't do to leave her, even for a moment."

How shrewd, thought Carol, reassessing Alice Fleming because she had immediately recognized the sting in the question. If the baby was likely to sleep right through it would be possible to leave her long enough to commit a murder.

Bourke came back with Charlie Date, and Alice stood as soon as he entered the trailer. "Inspector,

186

you won't be needing me anymore?" she said, shooting Charlie a glance that blended satisfaction and malice.

Charlie Date was subdued. "Of course this is about Helen," he said as Bourke gestured for him to be seated. "I knew her well and I'm so sorry to hear what's happened."

His regret was convincing, but Carol reminded herself that the person they were seeking must be a consummate actor. She said, "You were friends?"

"Not exactly. I worked for six months on *The Shipley Report* and had a lot to do with her. Helen was great to work with — efficient and stood no nonsense from anyone. I can't believe what's happened to her . . . she was the last person you'd think would be murdered."

Bourke was curious. "Why do you say that?"

"Because she always had everything under control. Knew where she was going, what was happening. How could she have let someone kill her?"

Bourke said, "What if it was a friend, an acquaintance . . . someone like you, for instance? She wouldn't be on her guard then."

Charlie didn't rise to Bourke's bait. "Maybe that's it," he said.

Bourke consulted papers. "You were with a counselor last night."

Carol was interested to see he looked down at the floor, apparently embarrassed. Bourke repeated the question.

"I heard you. I don't like my personal life being discussed."

"It's the matter of an alibi."

Charlie shoved a business card into Bourke's

hand. "Look, I don't want to talk about it. Ring him to check the appointment if you like. He'll tell you I was there from seven-thirty to eight-thirty."

Bourke passed the card to Carol. The address was within a few minutes' drive from the television station.

"Where did you go after the session ended?" he inquired.

"Home. Where else?"

"You live alone?"

For the first time strong emotion showed. "Oh yes," he said bitterly, "I live alone."

Vic Carbond had flatly refused to see them until the lunch break. He had spilt coffee down the front of his DEATH DOWN UNDER T-shirt and Carol wondered why he had chosen to wear white — some dark color would be in keeping with his personal habits.

"Come on, get on with it," he snarled. He glared at Carol. "I can tell you you're wasting your time — I can't tell you anything."

Bourke began the questioning, checking through Carbond's movements on the night Helen Tolsten died. Carbond snapped back answers, his impatience growing. "Look," he said, "the bloody barmaid remembers me being at the pub, doesn't she? That's all there is to it — I was there till late."

"The barmaid certainly does remember you," observed Carol, "no doubt because of your loud comments about her."

"Like all women," sneered Carbond, "can't take a joke. She's a slut, anyway."

Carol ignored his comment, saying, "What did you think of Helen Tolsten?"

188

"What's there to think? She was pushy — basked in Shipley's reflected glory. That's all I can say. I didn't have much to do with her."

Carbond admitted that Helen Tolsten had been liaising with him about Madeline Shipley's plans to visit *Death Down Under*'s Outback shooting sites, concluding with the comment, "I hardly knew her and didn't want to — she wasn't much of a looker, anyway."

After Carbond had made his surly departure, Bourke said, "That performance of his in the pub — it's almost as if he wanted the barmaid to notice him, isn't it?"

Chapter 15

By evening the wind of the morning had blown itself away, replaced with a drizzling rain that made the air thick and clammy. Standing beside Sybil as they jointly prepared dinner at the kitchen bench, Carol remarked, "I didn't see you at Harold Park today."

"I was busy educating in my little caravan."

Raising an eyebrow at her tone, Carol said, "Not a rewarding activity, I gather."

Sybil laughed ruefully. "Not with Malcolm Murtry, film star, in attendance. The attention you cops have been giving him has gone to his head, which has always been, I suspect, his weakest point. Today just keeping him in the caravan took most of my energy."

"So he's not worried about the possibility of being a suspect?"

Sybil chopped a zucchini with more than usual vehemence. "Malcolm would be more worried," she observed, "if he hadn't been included. He's one of those people who need to have an ego transfusion at regular intervals."

"You don't sound very fond of him."

Sybil considered the comment. "He's shallow, self-centered and egotistical. Apart from that, he's okay."

"What's he said about the murders?"

Sybil's expression showed distaste. "I think he finds them quite exciting . . . And he loved the lesbian element . . . kept on mentioning it until I shut him up."

Carol looked at her sideways and Sybil grinned. "Not by self-revelation, Carol. Rest easy, your secret is safe."

Carol sighed. "With Madeline in on the act, it may not be such a secret much longer."

Sybil had stopped attacking the vegetables and was watching her closely. "What can you do?"

Carol gave her a small smile. "Not much, I suppose. I just wait for the inevitable to happen." She added with mock cheerfulness, "And there could be advantages — I'm getting awfully tired of watching everything I say in case someone suspects something."

Sybil said carefully, "Do you want to talk about it?"

191

"Not particularly," said Carol honestly, "but I'll have to sooner or later. Let's do it after dinner." Carol flipped on the little portable television on the kitchen bench. "In the meantime, I'd like to catch my nemesis in action."

Madeline appeared on the screen in close-up. Her tailored black suit enhanced the warm copper of her hair. Her face was serious, almost tragic.

Fixing the camera with a steady gray gaze, she began. "Until this week, the shock and distress that continue to surround the murders of the Orange Strangler's victims was felt by myself and others associated with *The Shipley Report* keenly . . . but second-hand."

She paused, looked down. "But that is no longer the case . . ." Eyes up to the camera again, Madeline seemed moved almost to tears. "The fifth victim of the psychopathic killer is my colleague, my friend. Helen Tolsten died as she had lived — working to uncover the truth for you, the public . . . and her death was a dreadful one. I appeal to you to make sure it was not in vain."

"This is too much," said Sybil in disgust.

Carol was silent, watching as Madeline narrated the high points of Helen Tolsten's career, mentioning her fearless pursuit of the truth several times.

"Truth," said Sybil sarcastically, "has a rather elastic meaning when it comes to the media."

"Come out of the closet — is that what you're asking me to do?"

192

Sybil sighed in exasperation. "Carol, I'm not asking you to do anything. We're just supposed to be discussing the situation, so let's discuss it."

Carol threw up her hands. "It doesn't matter what I do, I'm going to lose. If I keep quiet, the word will eventually get out, people will start talking . . . And if I come right out and say I'm a lesbian . . ." She shook her head. "I don't know why I'm even considering that — I know I won't do it."

Watching Carol pace around the room, Sybil said, "I think it's a matter of personal pride. It's how you feel about yourself that's important — not what other people say or think."

Carol said furiously, "That's easy for you to say!"

"It's *not* easy to say," said Sybil vehemently, "but it's true. Carol, we're in the same boat. I'm a teacher, and there are some parents who'd be horrified to think a gay person, man or woman, could be teaching their children."

Carol thought, It's all too hard — but this time I can't ignore the issue. She sat down beside Sybil. "I've got a long way to go on this — I'm prepared to admit that. But, darling, you've got some way to go, also."

Sybil gave her a wan smile. "And ain't that the truth," she said.

Later, as they prepared for bed, Carol said, "Sybil, I love you."

"Thank you."

"Thank you? What does that mean?"

"It means I'm very grateful," said Sybil helpfully.

Carol lay back and laughed.

Sybil said, "What's so funny?"

"I am. You are."

With care she pulled Sybil down on top of her and began to kiss her, gently, thoroughly.

"What, no cave woman?" Sybil murmured against her mouth.

She made love slowly, carefully, considerately, taking the time to caress, kiss, hold. The urgent heat of desire was transformed, for the moment, into a deeper, melting, more comforting warmth.

She undressed Sybil without haste, sliding off her shirt, her jeans — feeling the intoxicating smoothness of skin under her palms, submitting to the voluptuous reward of being undressed in turn.

There was a point in love-making that always thrilled, delighted her . . . to have skin against skin, locked together, turning so that the full weight of the other woman pressed down against her body . . . that moment when all is promise, all is anticipation of what is to come.

Tonight she felt no concern whether she would climax or not. Her pleasure was in the pure sensual delight she could give, not take.

And her body rewarded her before she had realized what was happening. Her attention had been so concentrated upon Sybil tensing, arching under her caresses, quivering and then crying out her fulfillment as orgasm began, that Carol was caught unawares when she was overwhelmed and submerged in a matching release. It was a torrent of joy that went on and on, as wave after wave drowned her in obliterating sensation.

Spent, they lay in each other's arms. Carol thought drowsily that this was worth any hard decision she might have to make.

Just as she went to sleep the elusive memory nudged the edge of her consciousness. She could hear Mark Bourke saying, "A long time ago . . . remembered the face . . ." but before she could catch it and hold it she was asleep.

Chapter 16

Sybil brushed away a persistent fly, tilted her head to stop perspiration running into her eyes. Hummocks of spinifex grass thrust their needle-like leaves into the burning air, defying the parched glare of their pitiless environment. There was no shade, no movement, no clouds in the bleached pale sky. The heat was bouncing from the red earth and billowing against all of their sweating faces.

"Jesus," snarled Vic Carbond, "where the hell is Malcolm?"

The clump of people around the camera waited

patiently as Malcolm made his leisurely way from the group of vehicles that sustained them. Kirra skipped along beside him, unaffected by the ubiquitous red dust that covered clothes and skin in a gritty powder.

Sybil had found that any pretense of teaching had evaporated in the stinging heat. She wished she had something to do other than stand around and watch the interminable process of movie-making. At least the others could concentrate upon their individual functions and duties as a way of ignoring the hostility of the silent flat land that surrounded them.

Sybil squinted through her dark glasses that only mitigated the flat glare, but could not blunt it effectively. She thought longingly of the three previous days at Ayers Rock. Not only had they stayed in the cool luxury at an air-conditioned motel, but the whole experience of filming in Uluru National Park had been full of fascinating sights and experiences, made particularly significant by the huge red bulk of Ayers Rock itself, floating in the flat plain like a huge stone iceberg, its sandstone base submerged thousands of feet into the sea of sediment.

The move to the desert itself for the final location scenes had brought the harsh reality of the Outback much closer. They were in the center of a vast, under-populated continent, thousands of kilometers from the cool surge of the sea. Without the comforting cocoon of air-conditioned civilization it was easy to understand why so many of the early explorers had perished in the casual antagonism of these arid plains.

There was a beauty here, but it was an uncompromisingly harsh one. At night the Milky Way arched overhead in a brilliant and overwhelming display of familiar patterns made strange by its very brightness and by the myriad of stars previously hidden by the civilized glow of city lights.

At night in the desert, as the temperature dropped, Sybil always found herself looking up to find the Southern Cross. As a child she had been shown how to use the Cross to find true south and she always automatically followed this routine, fascinated by the fact that though the constellation wheeled in the sky, the formula always worked.

But now it was hard to imagine the coolness of darkness in the brassiness of the day. Sybil pulled her broad-brimmed hat down lower to protect her face and stood, resigned to discomfort, as the director took Kirra and Malcolm over and over their desperate stumbles through the huge circular clumps of spinifex grass.

"For God's sake, Malcolm, you're supposed to be near death from thirst! Not strolling down bloody Bondi Beach!"

In contrast to Vic Carbond's furious impatience, the rest of the crew showed an admirable stoicism. Luke grinned at her, the zinc cream on his lips and nose making him look like someone who should be in, or on, the cool blue sea. "Hot, eh?" he said. "Never mind, it'll soon be lunch."

Lunch was some relief because it provided a break from standing with the sun hammering neck and shoulders, but evening was the only time there was a chance to relax from the atavistic feeling that the land was a living entity that looked upon the invasion of strangers with malevolence.

For these final days of filming they were staying at a remote homestead, rough and uncomfortable by city standards, but an oasis of ease and delight in comparison with the red wastes of the desert. The isolation had drawn Sybil closer to the other members of the crew and each night after dinner she found herself drinking and laughing with them as though they had been together as a team for a long time. Even Charlie Date, who she had tended to avoid in Sydney, had become a friend with whom she chatted unselfconsciously.

The radio was tuned to a station in Alice Springs, and the newscasts seemed to Sybil to come from another world, so remote were the everyday items of sporting triumphs, natural disasters and political machinations from the harshly beautiful Outback environment.

The bleak landscape seemed to have affected Alice Fleming differently. She had become subdued and thoughtful, losing most of her usual boisterous gossiping enthusiasm and becoming watchfully silent.

Vic Carbond had announced the night before that Paul Crusoe and possibly Madeline Shipley would be joining them the next day, and early that morning as they assembled to leave for the location shooting, a dusty four-wheel drive had bumped down the rutted track to the homestead bearing the lanky body of the artist.

Sybil had never met him, but Carol had given a pungent description, so she was not surprised by his vague manner and crumpled khaki clothes. Alice sputtered to life at the advent of a celebrity, even if his status was only by virtue of his wife's fame.

"That's Paul Crusoe?" she said in obvious disappointment. "He's very ordinary looking, isn't he? Nondescript, really."

She dug Sybil in the ribs. "Of course, you know why he's here, don't you? Madeline had a bit on him in her show the other night about how he wants to do a series of paintings on the Aboriginal Dreamtime. Wonder when Madeline Shipley's arriving? She's doing a documentary, you know."

"She won't come out here," said Charlie scathingly. "Too bloody uncomfortable for someone like her."

Alice was indignant. "She's a professional, Madeline is. She wouldn't worry about a bit of heat and dust."

Charlie looked at Alice with superior contempt. "Madeline Shipley's a spoiled bitch," he said. "I should know . . . I've worked with her."

Chapter 17

Carol and Bourke were sitting in Bourke's office reviewing the latest information on the case. "Narelle Dent's the problem," he said, referring to the Orange Strangler's third victim. "Every other woman has some link to Shearing Media, but if there's one for Narelle Dent, I can't find it."

Two days before, on Monday, the television appearance Malcolm Murtry had remembered Narelle Dent making had been discovered. It had not been, to Bourke's chagrin, on Shearing's station, but on a competitor's. Narelle had been prominently featured in a news item as a shocked but beadily observant witness to a domestic argument and murder. Her next door neighbors, a couple with a turbulent and often violent relationship, had embarked upon a terminal fight.

The news clip had been retrieved from the channel's library and Carol had sat with Bourke and viewed it several times. Narelle had been auburn-haired, with pale blue, slightly protruding eyes, and a vivacious manner. She came over well on the screen, describing vividly her neighbors' raised voices, the shouts, the crashes of furniture, the husband chasing his screaming wife out the front door and the final shotgun murder and suicide.

The first time they watched it Bourke had said disapprovingly, "Bit of vulture, isn't she? She's really enjoying describing this."

Carol had agreed. Narelle Dent's effective description was accompanied by a disquieting glee as she detailed each stage of the double tragedy.

Now, looking at Bourke's frowning face, she said, "Those photographs of Alissa Harvey's — the ones of the Federation house — tell Ferguson to cross-check with domestic murder scenes. And did you get all of her other papers and photographs from her parents?"

He sketched a large outline in the air. "Boxes of them. Haven't had time to go through them in detail — just a glance."

"Put someone on it. I want any reference to domestic violence, particularly where there's a murder."

Bourke's frown deepened. "Why? What are you thinking?"

"I'm looking for the strangler's motive."

"Motive isn't important Carol," he protested. "It never is in these cases. The guy's a psychopath — he doesn't think in normal patterns."

She leaned forward to persuade him. "It *is* important — it's the key."

His tone indicated his reluctance to share her view. "So what's our strangler's motive, then?"

"It's something to do with the media's approach to violence."

Bourke protested, "If that were the case, he'd have motive enough to kill thousands, since blood, death and disaster are the staples of television and newspapers."

"One particular kind of violence triggers him."

"And he only kills women . . ."

"But what," said Carol, "if it's just that women are easier to kill?" She gestured at Bourke's neat printing on the whiteboards that covered two of his office walls. "We've been concentrating too much on the here and now, and not enough on the past. I want to know everything about the families these people came from. That's where the motive is, Mark. Something happened, something dreadful — and television and newspapers took the story and splashed it into public view."

She smiled at Bourke's resigned expression. "And one other thing, Mark, do you have the videotape Malcolm Murtry gave us of *Crime Time*?"

Bourke took the tape out of his desk and handed it to her. "Carol, the Fernandez case is a dead-end. I'm convinced there isn't a link to any of the suspects."

"It's not the Fernandez case," said Carol, "it's the one after it on the tape I'm interested in . . . something about it has been nagging at me."

He came back to her office and watched the video with her. She saw him lean forward, frowning, as the second program began. Before the dramatization of the crime a series of stills of the actual participants were shown.

"That's the familiar face," she said, freezing the frame. "We both recognized it."

"But it can't be him . . . he's dead."

"But did he kill his whole family?"

While Carol was snatching a sandwich and a cup of coffee for lunch the Commissioner's secretary called to say he wanted to see her in his office urgently. Carol sighed and complied.

She knew the Commissioner liked and admired her. He had always supported her, even when political considerations made it difficult, and, in turn, she was willing to keep him completely up to date with all details of investigations, trusting that nothing would be prematurely leaked to the media.

He came to the point immediately. "Wilbur Shearing's anxious. He has the impression he's somewhere near the head of the list of suspects for the serial strangler . . ."

"He was a suspect at one point, but no longer."

The Commissioner raised his photogenically heavy eyebrows. "Meaning?"

Carol explained the situation as she saw it. He listened intently, asking a couple of pointed questions when she had finished.

"Where is your main suspect at the moment?"

Suppressing the thrill of unease when she thought of Sybil, she said, "With *Death Down Under* in the desert somewhere between Ayers Rock and Alice Springs."

"And you don't think anyone's in any immediate danger?"

"No, but I don't think we can afford to wait until they finish and come back to Sydney, especially as I believe Madeline Shipley is the main target. With your permission I'll contact the Northern Territory police because, of course, we don't have jurisdiction . . ."

They discussed the legal situation, then, as she stood to leave, she said, "I think it's important the media don't get hold of this."

He nodded agreement. "I'll give Shearing the details, of course. It's his company, after all, and it's only fair he be prepared when it *does* hit the fan — but I'll make it absolutely clear nothing's to be leaked beforehand."

Carol wanted to object to Wilbur Shearing being told anything at all, but knew it would be futile, as the Commissioner and he were fast friends. She repeated how important it was to maintain a media blackout.

"I appreciate that, Carol, but when you do nail the Orange Strangler I think we can let all the stops out, don't you? God knows, the Force needs all the positive publicity it can get . . ."

Two hours later Bourke came to report. "Okay, Carol," he said, "we've hit pay dirt. Alissa Harvey has notes and photographs associated with a certain case twenty or so years ago, and, surprise, surprise, it just happens to be the one dramatized on *Crime Time*. The Federation house is in Mosman, and it was the family home."

He laid papers and photographs on her desk, handing her a magnifying glass. "Recognize anyone?"

"There's a strong family likeness."

"Sure is, and that's why we both thought we'd seen someone in the film crew who was familiar. Of course the name's changed."

With a flourish he put a dog-eared folder in front of her. "And I know you'll be impressed to find I've burrowed through the archives and found the original file on the case."

Even twenty years after the event Carol found the black and white photographs of a family's destruction moving. Roderick Forsythe had been the most successful television news personality of his time. His thin, handsome face, clear deep voice and air of authoritative concern were familiar to every viewer. He gave his channel's newscasts an advantage no competing station could match — a presenter who combined veracity and charisma. If Roderick Forsythe said it was so, countless viewers believed it to be true.

Looking at a photograph taken at the height of

his success, Carol wondered why no one had sensed the worm eating beneath the smooth skin of his persona, the madness that would drive him to destroy his family and himself.

One summer evening, twenty years ago, Roderick Forsythe had read the news with his customary skill, had his make-up removed and then driven home to his waiting family. The meal Freda Forsythe had prepared was never eaten. Her husband had systematically shot her and his three children, one by one, using a hunting rifle with cool efficiency. He had then put the barrel in his mouth and blown off the top of his handsome head.

One child, seriously wounded, had lived to give a statement of what had happened. To endure the pitiless glare of publicity as Forsythe's colleagues participated in a feeding frenzy of media sensationalism. And then, recovering, had faded from public sight.

Carol read through the statement taken beside the hospital bedside. The artless phrases — "And then Dad took the rifle and killed Mum . . . My brother was crying and screaming not to do it, but Dad shot him anyway . . ." — made her eyes sting with unexpected tears, but it was grief for the child who had survived, not for the monster he had become.

She cleared her throat, embarrassed that Bourke might notice. "Mark, arrange a charter flight tomorrow direct to Ayers Rock and a light plane to be waiting for us at the airport. I'll contact the Northern Territory authorities to ensure we have an officer to go with us."

Chapter 18

Sybil was up at first light, if for no other reason than to enjoy the merciful coolness before the brazen red sun leaped up from the horizon to fry the red land in another burning day.

Alice met her in the kitchen as she made a mug of coffee. "Just heard the early news, dear! They've got the Orange Strangler!"

Charlie, who had followed her in, said, "Who is it, then?"

Not bothering to hide her dislike, Alice snapped, "Well, I don't know, do I? Don't think they've actually *arrested* him yet, but they're close, or they wouldn't have let the news out and warned him, would they?"

"Fucking reporters will do anything that suits them," said Charlie.

Vic scowled his way into the spartan room. "Jesus, someone get me a coffee. As if I didn't have enough to worry about, they've just told me on the radio telephone that Madeline Shipley and company are landing here in a light aircraft this morning."

Mark Bourke hated air travel, so he was tardy arriving at the airport and he hurried up the stairs of the charter plane at the last moment. Carol knew that it was fear that silenced him as the plane trembled with anticipation, skimmed along the runway and, taking a deep breath, launched itself into the air. When he seemed finally convinced by the rapidly receding red tile roofs of Sydney that the plane was not about to fall out of the sky, he said to Carol, "Heard the news on the radio this morning? Some bastard's broken the story."

Carol gave a brief nod. "The source was almost certainly Shearing. The Commissioner insisted on telling him, in confidence of course, what was happening. The only good thing is he didn't mention specific names — probably holding that scoop for his own outlets."

"That fits in with Madeline Shipley."

She frowned at him. "What do you mean?"

"Ferguson rang me before I left this morning. He had an early appointment to see Madeline at the

209

channel to clear up some details about Helen Tolsten's normal routine. When he arrived, he discovered she wasn't there. Seems that yesterday afternoon she suddenly ups and flies to Ayers Rock. What do you make of that, eh?"

Carol let her breath out in a long sigh. "She knows an arrest is imminent and she wants to be in for the kill."

Bourke smiled grimly. "Well, let's hope the kill isn't her."

The plane droned across a landscape that had become less and less marked by civilization as they progressed. The sheer immensity of the scarred land seemed to make Bourke uncomfortable. He turned his head away from the monotony of the dry contours. "Helen Tolsten must have been killed outside Madeline's place."

Carol looked up from her contemplation of the blurred blue distance. She had been assuring herself that her judgment was right — that Sybil was safe because of what she had experienced in the past.

"Sorry?"

He repeated the statement.

Carol was happy to concentrate her thoughts on something other than worrying about Sybil. "I'm sure you're right, Mark. Helen was an employee, so Paul and Madeline didn't see her off. She said goodnight, went out to her car, was strangled efficiently, probably before she had the faintest idea anything was wrong. Her car with her body in it was driven, I think, to the murderer's garage, and there she was transferred to a van. Much later her car, with a light motorcycle in the trunk, was taken to the street outside Shearing's television channel, the motorbike was lifted out and left to provide transport back to her body, and the car driven in to be found the next day in the car park."

"Why run a chance of being seen? The car could have been dumped anywhere."

Carol smiled grimly. "I think the killer did it to confuse — a devious gesture to puzzle the stupid cops."

Vic Carbond raised his head at the burring sound. "Shipley's arrived," he said sourly.

Sybil watched the light plane bounce along the rutted landing strip, thinking it looked more like an insubstantial toy than an efficient means of transport.

Paul Crusoe went to meet his wife, who emerged looking cool and competent in a broadbrimmed hat, shorts and a long-sleeved shirt as protection against the sun.

Ignoring the fact that she might need refreshment after her flight from the Rock, Carbond began hectoring her immediately. He had to shout above the noise of the plane, which had disgorged luggage and Madeline's cameraman and was turning to take off again. "Come on, Madeline," he bellowed, "we've been wasting time waiting for you. If you want to be on the shoot, you've got to come right now."

Luke was bent over the radio, listening. Vic Carbond nudged him roughly. "We're ready."

Sybil rode with Malcolm, Kirra, Luke and his assistant in the generator truck which had an air-conditioned cabin. Luke drove, as he did everything, neatly, cleanly and with the minimum of fuss.

She was sitting beside him and he leaned over to say above the roar of the engine, "Don't let Madeline Shipley get too close to you. She's a shark. She'll rip out your guts and smile as she does it. You know what it's like already, you've been through it . . . the way they twist the truth and show private things to the world."

"Luke, I'm not news any more. She wouldn't bother."

As they bumped to a stop at the site, he said, "Don't count on it. They love raking over the coals, resurrecting old tragedies. All of them, they're parasites."

By late afternoon everyone was hot and irritable. Clouds of flies combined with the scorching heat to make conditions almost intolerable and the usual smooth functioning of the crew was absent. Even Alice was moved to snap impatiently at Kirra over a costume change.

The only person unmoved by the trying conditions was Madeline. The cameraman she had brought with her followed her around glumly as she filmed short interviews with different members of the crew when they were available from their duties.

Although Sybil felt a scornful dislike for Madeline, as part of the film crew she felt obliged to agree to an interview. Madeline, all smiling charm, asked a series of questions about tutoring children on a film set in the middle of the Outback. Sybil tried to

212

answer truthfully, but tactfully, suspecting that the Education Department would not be impressed by total candor.

The day dragged to a hot and sticky end. Everyone was relieved to bump their way back to the comparative comfort of the homestead buildings.

It was nearing dusk when the faint drone of an aircraft stopped conversation on the wide veranda where drinks and a gentle evening breeze made life bearable.

Alice's curiosity was unquenchable. "Who could that be, way out here?" she said, craning her neck to see the plane.

The distant speck grew larger, assumed wings and a fuselage, drifted lower in the cooling evening air. "Got to be coming here," declared Alice, "there's nowhere else to go."

People stood, moved around, as if disturbed by the unexpected visitation. Sybil watched a repeat performance of the morning's landing, but this time when the craft juddered to rest at the end of the runway near the homestead the propeller stopped also.

She saw the slim body, decisive movements and sheen of straight blonde hair and realized with astonishment that the first person stepping swiftly out of the aircraft was Carol. She was followed by two men. One was Mark Bourke, the other a stranger.

Vic Carbond tramped out to meet them, his shoulders set truculently. Sybil watched them confer and noticed with interest Vic's aggressive stance change. He shook his head, looked back over his shoulder, and called out to Malcolm, who was hovering nearby in an attempt to hear what was going on.

Dispatched with second-hand authority, Malcolm announced to Sybil and those near her, "Vic wants us all together in the main room, okay? Now!"

He marched off with his message as Carol, Bourke and the third man, who Sybil suddenly noticed was carrying a rifle down by his side, walked rapidly over to the main house.

Carol gave Sybil a brief, private smile as she passed her, Mark Bourke greeted her with a slight nod.

The crew were straggling into the house when Paul Crusoe called out. "Madeline! Where is she? Has anybody seen her?"

As he spoke an engine roared and a truck came careening over the bumpy ground heading straight for the fragile outline of the little plane. Sybil watched in open-mouthed amazement. The wing bent and splintered as the heavy metal mudguard lifted the body of the aircraft, leaving it stricken and broken. The truck reversed, trying to free itself from the wreckage which clung obstinately to the heavy metal grille protecting its engine.

The man with the rifle, Sybil saw, was running with purpose. When he was in position he slowed to a stop, raised the rifle and snapped off several shots. The truck lurched and settled as its tires deflated.

The driver turned off the engine, and in the sudden silence Bourke said, "Get back, all of you."

Carol walked unhurriedly towards the crippled vehicle, stopping beside the man with the rifle. He spoke out, his voice seeming unnaturally loud, announcing his name and rank in the Northern

Territory police force. As he began the official caution the door of the cab was pushed open and Madeline, her face contorted with terror, began to climb down.

Stepping nimbly beside her, one hand clutching her shoulder, was Luke West. In his other hand was a knife that gleamed wickedly in the dying light as he held it against the side of Madeline's throat.

"I'll kill her," he warned. His voice was calm, conversational. He positioned himself carefully behind her, his back to the truck.

Carol's voice was similarly unemotional. "You're intending to murder her anyway, aren't you?"

Luke's teeth showed in a smile. "So you know all about it, Inspector — why I had to do it."

Carol took a step forward and Madeline cried out as Luke pushed the point of the knife into her neck. "No closer. I'll have to ask someone to replace a distributor cap in one of the other trucks. I disabled them — didn't know I'd be needing them again."

Sybil was held, with the others, in a frozen tableau. Her eyes caught a slight movement and she realized that Bourke had faded back when the confrontation had begun and was now making a huge circle in an effort to get behind Luke and his hostage.

Carol said, "I'm afraid your Aunt Bea let you down."

For the first time anger showed in his voice. He glared at Carol. "Never, she'd never do that!"

She had his full attention as she shrugged regretfully. "Of course she told us you called in to see her the night you killed Helen Tolsten, but you went out again for an hour, saying you had to get a part for her light switch. And you drove straight to

215

where you knew Helen was having dinner and you killed her as she went to get into her car in the driveway."

Luke ignored what she had said. "Auntie Bea wouldn't betray me. She always said I was her son."

Carol said brutally, "But you're the son of a madman, aren't you, Luke? Someone who shot the members of his family, one by one."

Madeline whimpered as he shoved her forward. "It's people like her that made him do it!"

Carol made a derisive sound. "No one *made* your father a murderer — he was insane."

Staring wide-eyed at Carol, Luke twisted the point of the knife until blood began to run down Madeline's neck. Above her cry of pain he shouted, "I'm not listening to this! Get me another truck or I'll cut her throat, right now, in front of you!"

Carol held out a length of orange cord. "Sure you wouldn't rather strangle her?"

His eyes fixed on the bright cord, Luke didn't see the movement behind him. There was no struggle. Bourke was, as always, efficient, disarming him with quick skill.

Luke lifted his handcuffed wrists, saying in a tone of mild complaint, "This isn't really necessary, you know. There's nowhere for me to go."

"Humor us," said Bourke, with a sideways glance at Carol.

Bourke had chosen one of the smaller rooms in the building because it had only one narrow window and a door that could be locked. Carol could hear the

216

distant, steady beat of the generator that fed the homestead lights. She said, "We have some questions."

Luke leaned back in his chair, relaxed, his hands folded in his lap. "What do you want to know?"

Bourke matched Luke's conversational tone. "How about Helen Tolsten?"

"I wanted Madeline Shipley that night — that's who I was there for — but her husband was in the way, so I decided to make do with Helen. She was just as guilty, anyway."

"Guilty of what?" queried Carol.

Luke looked at her, his head tilted to one side. "You know what it is. I know you understand. They poison people's minds and drive them mad."

Carol sounded sympathetic. "That happened to your father?"

"Yes! He wouldn't have done it otherwise — he loved us all very much."

Bourke asked, "Why the orange rope?"

Luke shrugged, grinned. "I liked the color." He became more serious when Carol asked him about the laying out of the bodies. "I had to do that — once they'd died they'd atoned for their sins." He rubbed his knuckles across his chin. "You see, don't you? I owed it to them to make them acceptable to God, so I took off their clothes and hid their faces. But God had to know they'd been punished, too, so it was necessary to tie the feet and hands, and knot a loop of rope around the throat."

Luke moved suddenly, bringing Bourke to his feet. Luke grinned up at him. "Give you a fright, did I?" He watched Bourke seat himself, then said to Carol, "I shut off their lying voices, closed their throats."

217

Showing none of the chill horror she felt, Carol said, "Tell us about it."

"They thrash around," he said, as though discussing some mundane topic, "so you have to hold the rope tight and stand well back. Two of them I did in cars and that was easy. I just said I had to get something from the back seat, slid in behind them, looped the rope around their necks and pulled their heads back over the seat."

Luke paused, as if for approbation. He stared into Carol's eyes. She felt an impulse to draw back, but she didn't move. Her thoughts were disconnected: You're not human . . . You're like a pitiless machine . . . I'd destroy you if I could . . .

"Before I do it," said Luke, "I like to let them have a hint of what's going to happen, so I can see the beginning of fear in their eyes . . . and then I hear them take their last breath. It wheezes in their throats as I tighten the rope . . ."

Chapter 19

In the cool night the Milky Way, thick with a million constellations, arched overhead.

"Luke was kind to me," said Sybil as she and Carol walked in the starlight. "I can hardly believe he's a killer."

"Luke wouldn't have hurt you, I'm sure of that. He saw you as someone who had suffered, as he had, from the media."

"But it's not enough, Carol — not enough to make someone kill five people. Did he tell you all about it?"

Luke's calm descriptions had filled Carol's imagination with hideous images — and sounds. It was something she would never share with Sybil. "Luke's happy to have an audience. He's still talking to Mark."

They walked in silence. After a while Sybil said, "There's something I've been meaning to say."

Carol stopped. "Will I want to hear it?"

"Could be," said Sybil. "It's that I love you."

Carol took her hands. "And? Isn't there something you should add? Something about never leaving?"

Sybil reflected. "Well," she said, "I'm not planning to . . . at least not in the foreseeable future, that is."

A few of the publications of
THE NAIAD PRESS, INC.
P.O. Box 10543 ● Tallahassee, Florida 32302
Phone (904) 539-5965
Mail orders welcome. Please include 15% postage.

DEATH DOWN UNDER by Claire McNab. 240 pp. 3rd Det. Insp. Carol Ashton mystery.　　　　ISBN 0-941483-39-8　　$8.95

MONTANA FEATHERS by Penny Hayes. 256 pp. Vivian and Elizabeth find love in frontier Montana.　　ISBN 0-941483-61-4　　8.95

CHESAPEAKE PROJECT by Phyllis Horn. 304 pp. Jessie & Meredith in perilous adventure.　　ISBN 0-941483-58-4　　8.95

LIFESTYLES by Jackie Calhoun. 224 pp. Contemporary Lesbian lives and loves.　　　　ISBN 0-941483-57-6　　8.95

VIRAGO by Karen Marie Christa Minns. 208 pp. Darsen has chosen Ginny.　　　　ISBN 0-941483-56-8　　8.95

WILDERNESS TREK by Dorothy Tell. 192 pp. Six women on vacation learning "new" skills.　　ISBN 0-941483-60-6　　8.95

MURDER BY THE BOOK by Pat Welch. 256 pp. A Helen Black Mystery. First in a series.　　ISBN 0-941483-59-2　　8.95

BERRIGAN by Vicki P. McConnell. 176 pp. Youthful Lesbian–romantic, idealistic Berrigan.　　ISBN 0-941483-55-X　　8.95

LESBIANS IN GERMANY by Lillian Faderman & B. Eriksson. 128 pp. Fiction, poetry, essays.　　ISBN 0-941483-62-2　　8.95

THE BEVERLY MALIBU by Katherine V. Forrest. 288 pp. A Kate Delafield Mystery. 3rd in a series.　　ISBN 0-941483-47-9　　16.95

THERE'S SOMETHING I'VE BEEN MEANING TO TELL YOU Ed. by Loralee MacPike. 288 pp. Gay men and lesbians coming out to their children.　　ISBN 0-941483-44-4　　9.95
　　　　　　　　　　　　　　　ISBN 0-941483-54-1　　16.95

LIFTING BELLY by Gertrude Stein. Ed. by Rebecca Mark. 104 pp. Erotic poetry.　　　　ISBN 0-941483-51-7　　8.95
　　　　　　　　　　　　　　　ISBN 0-941483-53-3　　14.95

ROSE PENSKI by Roz Perry. 192 pp. Adult lovers in a long-term relationship.　　　　ISBN 0-941483-37-1　　8.95

AFTER THE FIRE by Jane Rule. 256 pp. Warm, human novel by this incomparable author.　　ISBN 0-941483-45-2　　8.95

SUE SLATE, PRIVATE EYE by Lee Lynch. 176 pp. The gay folk of Peacock Alley are *all* cats.　　ISBN 0-941483-52-5　　8.95

CHRIS by Randy Salem. 224 pp. Golden oldie. Handsome Chris and her adventures.　　　　ISBN 0-941483-42-8　　8.95

THREE WOMEN by March Hastings. 232 pp. Golden oldie. A triangle among wealthy sophisticates.　　ISBN 0-941483-43-6　　8.95

RICE AND BEANS by Valeria Taylor. 232 pp. Love and
romance on poverty row. ISBN 0-941483-41-X   8.95

PLEASURES by Robbi Sommers. 204 pp. Unprecedented
eroticism. ISBN 0-941483-49-5   8.95

EDGEWISE by Camarin Grae. 372 pp. Spellbinding
adventure. ISBN 0-941483-19-3   9.95

FATAL REUNION by Claire McNab. 216 pp. 2nd Det. Inspec.
Carol Ashton mystery. ISBN 0-941483-40-1   8.95

KEEP TO ME STRANGER by Sarah Aldridge. 372 pp. Romance
set in a department store dynasty. ISBN 0-941483-38-X   9.95

HEARTSCAPE by Sue Gambill. 204 pp. American lesbian in
Portugal. ISBN 0-941483-33-9   8.95

IN THE BLOOD by Lauren Wright Douglas. 252 pp. Lesbian
science fiction adventure fantasy ISBN 0-941483-22-3   8.95

THE BEE'S KISS by Shirley Verel. 216 pp. Delicate, delicious
romance. ISBN 0-941483-36-3   8.95

RAGING MOTHER MOUNTAIN by Pat Emmerson. 264 pp.
Furosa Firechild's adventures in Wonderland. ISBN 0-941483-35-5   8.95

IN EVERY PORT by Karin Kallmaker. 228 pp. Jessica's sexy,
adventuresome travels. ISBN 0-941483-37-7   8.95

OF LOVE AND GLORY by Evelyn Kennedy. 192 pp. Exciting
WWII romance. ISBN 0-941483-32-0   8.95

CLICKING STONES by Nancy Tyler Glenn. 288 pp. Love
transcending time. ISBN 0-941483-31-2   8.95

SURVIVING SISTERS by Gail Pass. 252 pp. Powerful love
story. ISBN 0-941483-16-9   8.95

SOUTH OF THE LINE by Catherine Ennis. 216 pp. Civil War
adventure. ISBN 0-941483-29-0   8.95

WOMAN PLUS WOMAN by Dolores Klaich. 300 pp. Supurb
Lesbian overview. ISBN 0-941483-28-2   9.95

SLOW DANCING AT MISS POLLY'S by Sheila Ortiz Taylor.
96 pp. Lesbian Poetry ISBN 0-941483-30-4   7.95

DOUBLE DAUGHTER by Vicki P. McConnell. 216 pp. A Nyla
Wade Mystery, third in the series. ISBN 0-941483-26-6   8.95

HEAVY GILT by Delores Klaich. 192 pp. Lesbian detective/
disappearing homophobes/upper class gay society.
ISBN 0-941483-25-8   8.95

THE FINER GRAIN by Denise Ohio. 216 pp. Brilliant young
college lesbian novel. ISBN 0-941483-11-8   8.95

THE AMAZON TRAIL by Lee Lynch. 216 pp. Life, travel & lore
of famous lesbian author. ISBN 0-941483-27-4   8.95

DUSTY'S QUEEN OF HEARTS DINER by Lee Lynch. 240 pp.
Romantic blue-collar novel.   ISBN 0-941483-01-0   8.95

PARENTS MATTER by Ann Muller. 240 pp. Parents'
relationships with Lesbian daughters and gay sons.
                                          ISBN 0-930044-91-6   9.95

THE PEARLS by Shelley Smith. 176 pp. Passion and fun in
the Caribbean sun.   ISBN 0-930044-93-2   7.95

MAGDALENA by Sarah Aldridge. 352 pp. Epic Lesbian novel
set on three continents.   ISBN 0-930044-99-1   8.95

THE BLACK AND WHITE OF IT by Ann Allen Shockley.
144 pp. Short stories.   ISBN 0-930044-96-7   7.95

SAY JESUS AND COME TO ME by Ann Allen Shockley. 288
pp. Contemporary romance.   ISBN 0-930044-98-3   8.95

LOVING HER by Ann Allen Shockley. 192 pp. Romantic love
story.   ISBN 0-930044-97-5   7.95

MURDER AT THE NIGHTWOOD BAR by Katherine V.
Forrest. 240 pp. A Kate Delafield mystery. Second in a series.
                                          ISBN 0-930044-92-4   8.95

ZOE'S BOOK by Gail Pass. 224 pp. Passionate, obsessive love
story.   ISBN 0-930044-95-9   7.95

WINGED DANCER by Camarin Grae. 228 pp. Erotic Lesbian
adventure story.   ISBN 0-930044-88-6   8.95

PAZ by Camarin Grae. 336 pp. Romantic Lesbian adventurer
with the power to change the world.   ISBN 0-930044-89-4   8.95

SOUL SNATCHER by Camarin Grae. 224 pp. A puzzle, an
adventure, a mystery — Lesbian romance.   ISBN 0-930044-90-8   8.95

THE LOVE OF GOOD WOMEN by Isabel Miller. 224 pp.
Long-awaited new novel by the author of the beloved *Patience
and Sarah*.   ISBN 0-930044-81-9   8.95

THE HOUSE AT PELHAM FALLS by Brenda Weathers. 240
pp. Suspenseful Lesbian ghost story.   ISBN 0-930044-79-7   7.95

HOME IN YOUR HANDS by Lee Lynch. 240 pp. More stories
from the author of *Old Dyke Tales*.   ISBN 0-930044-80-0   7.95

EACH HAND A MAP by Anita Skeen. 112 pp. Real-life poems
that touch us all.   ISBN 0-930044-82-7   6.95

SURPLUS by Sylvia Stevenson. 342 pp. A classic early Lesbian
novel.   ISBN 0-930044-78-9   7.95

PEMBROKE PARK by Michelle Martin. 256 pp. Derring-do
and daring romance in Regency England.   ISBN 0-930044-77-0   7.95

THE LONG TRAIL by Penny Hayes. 248 pp. Vivid adventures
of two women in love in the old west.   ISBN 0-930044-76-2   8.95

HORIZON OF THE HEART by Shelley Smith. 192 pp. Hot
romance in summertime New England.   ISBN 0-930044-75-4   7.95

AN EMERGENCE OF GREEN by Katherine V. Forrest. 288
pp. Powerful novel of sexual discovery.   ISBN 0-930044-69-X   8.95

THE LESBIAN PERIODICALS INDEX edited by Claire
Potter. 432 pp. Author & subject index.   ISBN 0-930044-74-6   29.95

DESERT OF THE HEART by Jane Rule. 224 pp. A classic;
basis for the movie *Desert Hearts.*   ISBN 0-930044-73-8   7.95

SPRING FORWARD/FALL BACK by Sheila Ortiz Taylor.
288 pp. Literary novel of timeless love.   ISBN 0-930044-70-3   7.95

FOR KEEPS by Elisabeth Nonas. 144 pp. Contemporary novel
about losing and finding love.   ISBN 0-930044-71-1   7.95

TORCHLIGHT TO VALHALLA by Gale Wilhelm. 128 pp.
Classic novel by a great Lesbian writer.   ISBN 0-930044-68-1   7.95

LESBIAN NUNS: BREAKING SILENCE edited by Rosemary
Curb and Nancy Manahan. 432 pp. Unprecedented autobiographies
of religious life.   ISBN 0-930044-62-2   9.95

THE SWASHBUCKLER by Lee Lynch. 288 pp. Colorful novel
set in Greenwich Village in the sixties.   ISBN 0-930044-66-5   8.95

MISFORTUNE'S FRIEND by Sarah Aldridge. 320 pp. Histori-
cal Lesbian novel set on two continents.   ISBN 0-930044-67-3   7.95

A STUDIO OF ONE'S OWN by Ann Stokes. Edited by
Dolores Klaich. 128 pp. Autobiography.   ISBN 0-930044-64-9   7.95

SEX VARIANT WOMEN IN LITERATURE by Jeannette
Howard Foster. 448 pp. Literary history.   ISBN 0-930044-65-7   8.95

A HOT-EYED MODERATE by Jane Rule. 252 pp. Hard-hitting
essays on gay life; writing; art.   ISBN 0-930044-57-6   7.95

INLAND PASSAGE AND OTHER STORIES by Jane Rule.
288 pp. Wide-ranging new collection.   ISBN 0-930044-56-8   7.95

WE TOO ARE DRIFTING by Gale Wilhelm. 128 pp. Timeless
Lesbian novel, a masterpiece.   ISBN 0-930044-61-4   6.95

AMATEUR CITY by Katherine V. Forrest. 224 pp. A Kate
Delafield mystery. First in a series.   ISBN 0-930044-55-X   8.95

THE SOPHIE HOROWITZ STORY by Sarah Schulman. 176
pp. Engaging novel of madcap intrigue.   ISBN 0-930044-54-1   7.95

THE BURNTON WIDOWS by Vickie P. McConnell. 272 pp. A
Nyla Wade mystery, second in the series.   ISBN 0-930044-52-5   7.95

OLD DYKE TALES by Lee Lynch. 224 pp. Extraordinary
stories of our diverse Lesbian lives.   ISBN 0-930044-51-7   8.95

DAUGHTERS OF A CORAL DAWN by Katherine V. Forrest.
240 pp. Novel set in a Lesbian new world.   ISBN 0-930044-50-9   8.95

THE PRICE OF SALT by Claire Morgan. 288 pp. A milestone
novel, a beloved classic. ISBN 0-930044-49-5 8.95

AGAINST THE SEASON by Jane Rule. 224 pp. Luminous,
complex novel of interrelationships. ISBN 0-930044-48-7 8.95

LOVERS IN THE PRESENT AFTERNOON by Kathleen
Fleming. 288 pp. A novel about recovery and growth.
ISBN 0-930044-46-0 8.95

TOOTHPICK HOUSE by Lee Lynch. 264 pp. Love between
two Lesbians of different classes. ISBN 0-930044-45-2 7.95

MADAME AURORA by Sarah Aldridge. 256 pp. Historical
novel featuring a charismatic "seer." ISBN 0-930044-44-4 7.95

CURIOUS WINE by Katherine V. Forrest. 176 pp. Passionate
Lesbian love story, a best-seller. ISBN 0-930044-43-6 8.95

BLACK LESBIAN IN WHITE AMERICA by Anita Cornwell.
141 pp. Stories, essays, autobiography. ISBN 0-930044-41-X 7.95

CONTRACT WITH THE WORLD by Jane Rule. 340 pp.
Powerful, panoramic novel of gay life. ISBN 0-930044-28-2 9.95

MRS. PORTER'S LETTER by Vicki P. McConnell. 224 pp.
The first Nyla Wade mystery. ISBN 0-930044-29-0 7.95

TO THE CLEVELAND STATION by Carol Anne Douglas.
192 pp. Interracial Lesbian love story. ISBN 0-930044-27-4 6.95

THE NESTING PLACE by Sarah Aldridge. 224 pp. A
three-woman triangle—love conquers all! ISBN 0-930044-26-6 7.95

THIS IS NOT FOR YOU by Jane Rule. 284 pp. A letter to a
beloved is also an intricate novel. ISBN 0-930044-25-8 8.95

FAULTLINE by Sheila Ortiz Taylor. 140 pp. Warm, funny,
literate story of a startling family. ISBN 0-930044-24-X 6.95

THE LESBIAN IN LITERATURE by Barbara Grier. 3d ed.
Foreword by Maida Tilchen. 240 pp. Comprehensive bibliography.
Literary ratings; rare photos. ISBN 0-930044-23-1 7.95

ANNA'S COUNTRY by Elizabeth Lang. 208 pp. A woman
finds her Lesbian identity. ISBN 0-930044-19-3 6.95

PRISM by Valerie Taylor. 158 pp. A love affair between two
women in their sixties. ISBN 0-930044-18-5 6.95

BLACK LESBIANS: AN ANNOTATED BIBLIOGRAPHY
compiled by J. R. Roberts. Foreword by Barbara Smith. 112 pp.
Award-winning bibliography. ISBN 0-930044-21-5 5.95

THE MARQUISE AND THE NOVICE by Victoria Ramstetter.
108 pp. A Lesbian Gothic novel. ISBN 0-930044-16-9 6.95

OUTLANDER by Jane Rule. 207 pp. Short stories and essays
by one of our finest writers. ISBN 0-930044-17-7 8.95

ALL TRUE LOVERS by Sarah Aldridge. 292 pp. Romantic
novel set in the 1930s and 1940s.   ISBN 0-930044-10-X   7.95

A WOMAN APPEARED TO ME by Renee Vivien. 65 pp. A
classic; translated by Jeannette H. Foster.   ISBN 0-930044-06-1   5.00

CYTHEREA'S BREATH by Sarah Aldridge. 240 pp. Romantic
novel about women's entrance into medicine.
                                              ISBN 0-930044-02-9   6.95

TOTTIE by Sarah Aldridge. 181 pp. Lesbian romance in the
turmoil of the sixties.   ISBN 0-930044-01-0   6.95

THE LATECOMER by Sarah Aldridge. 107 pp. A delicate love
story.   ISBN 0-930044-00-2   6.95

ODD GIRL OUT by Ann Bannon.   ISBN 0-930044-83-5   5.95

I AM A WOMAN by Ann Bannon.   ISBN 0-930044-84-3   5.95

WOMEN IN THE SHADOWS by Ann Bannon.
                                              ISBN 0-930044-85-1   5.95

JOURNEY TO A WOMAN by Ann Bannon.
                                              ISBN 0-930044-86-X   5.95

BEEBO BRINKER by Ann Bannon.   ISBN 0-930044-87-8   5.95
          Legendary novels written in the fifties and sixties,
               set in the gay mecca of Greenwich Village.

VOLUTE BOOKS

JOURNEY TO FULFILLMENT   Early classics by Valerie   3.95

A WORLD WITHOUT MEN   Taylor: The Erika Frohmann   3.95

RETURN TO LESBOS   series.   3.95

These are just a few of the many Naiad Press titles — we are the oldest and
largest lesbian/feminist publishing company in the world. Please request a
complete catalog. We offer personal service; we encourage and welcome
direct mail orders from individuals who have limited access to bookstores
carrying our publications.